Changing the World
By Education at Table

CHANGING THE WORLD BY EDUCATION AT TABLE

CULTURE DIFFERENCE & COMMUNITY BOND

Clara Soonhee Kwon-Tatum, Ph.D

Macro Education Instute, INC

Recommendations

> I expect 『Changing the World by Education at Table』 to be a guide in quenching the thirst for education in building a good character, especially, trustworthiness, respect for others, responsibility, fairness, caring, and good citizenship. The author, who has had the unique experience of having been an educator in both Korea and America, enlightens us through this book about the concept of dinner table education; this stems from an ideology present in ancient dignitary households, called Sik-Shi-Oh-Gwan(식시오관), which means to think of five things to be grateful for while eating food. This is the great Korean way of teaching, and it covers lessons for our minds, morals, and bodies. It teaches us that it should be the basis for saving the collapsing character education of now. Furthermore, the book's ability to identify and analyze problems in racially divisive America serves as a compass for Korea as it evolves from a homogenous to a diverse nation.

— Young-Mi Lee | Educator, Education Administrator

> This is a hybrid book. The essays in it power the Korean and American hearts simultaneously. The title, *Changing the World by*

V

Education at Table, penetrates both hearts. I further recommend reading this book, as current dinner table education looks different from what it used to look like.

— Hong-Gyu Chung | Author, Professor

> The author seems to present a profound alternative needed in our lives through the framework of rationality and shining insight from her mental poise and structural thinking. She also looks at the world with a deep understanding of people and is knowledgeable in history, politics, social issues, and culture. Her knowledge and advice are the principles of pure love; she will contribute deeply as a landmark of education.

— Moses Choi | Musician, Essayist

> The author's voice gets clearer and her emotions more vivid when she speaks of the cultural alienation and differences she runs across in an unfamiliar environment. Her voice, strengthened by her experiences, pierces through the volume of reality. The echo of empathy amplifies by her sharp insight on issues such as education and translation.

— Suk-Ju Chang | Poet, Literary Critic

Preface

Learning about and understanding other people are difficult. To understand other people who live in vastly different cultures and societies are even more challenging. The advances of the Internet have made accessing information from different cultures easier, but experiencing the locals' laughter, tears, sweat, and breath (at times calm, others labored) in the flesh is not an easy feat. Perhaps this is why many people enjoy traveling. Even while traveling, however, it is still not easy to learn and understand the locals' inner lives. Through this book, I wanted to satisfy the readers' yearning for learning about the sounds of the locals' breaths as well as delve into the suffering of Korean immigrants as minorities in a foreign country.

The impetus for writing this book came from discovering and researching the deep-rooted issue of low high school graduation rates in America. The statistic that the majority did not graduate from a public high school in large metropolitan cities revealed to me the reality of the dark side of the American public education system. Further, the abundant institutional aids were nothing more than a showy gimmick disguising the sad truth of students abandoning the school. The American educational system provides astronomical financial aid and free required education to public schools in large cities, but students have chosen to drop out of school for decades.

I had known about statistics as such, given my experience of teaching English in South Korea, but I did not understand the full extent of this ironic phenomenon until I moved overseas and lived alongside the American locals. Particularly, with my experience of growing up and teaching in South Korea, I found the cause of this issue outside of the American education system; the main issue behind the failure of the system and dropouts stems from the deep-rooted issue with the contradictive nature of the educational framework itself. I learned that there were social, cultural, and political facets all interconnected in the school system through my experience abroad.

With the unique experience of working in the educational field in both South Korea and America up my sleeve, I saw the American social, cultural, and political systems through an educational lens. I thoroughly investigated the lives of the American working class and minorities, and in doing so, I rediscovered the Korean heritage and pride persevering so far away from home. The prestige of South Korean companies in America and the morals and values of Korean culture especially tell us that the size of a country or the economy of its educational system are inconsequential. The greatness of South Korea was built on the culture created by our ancestors and the legacy of our cultural, social, and political heritage on which the high quality of our educational system and our dinner table education are based. Koreans' consistent frugality and diligence lead to us quietly letting ourselves be known all over the world, making us true patriots and diplomats.

This book, *Changing The World by Education at Table*, starts with the hope that with dinner table education existent in every Korean household, any problem of the American educational system can be fixed to a degree. Fortunately, in 2009, President Obama tried to solve the root problem that no education professional, politician, or president in history was able to. He focused on kindergarten, preschool, and afterschool education, similar to the ideology of the Korean dinner table education, and alongside an enormous budget, led the reform on the political, cultural, and social aspects of education, bringing about educational reform in America. These were revolutionary measures that solved the deep-rooted issues persistent in low-income people of large cities. The lessons and positive expectations parents instill in their children morning and night can raise the self-esteem of children, strengthening their perseverance and patience. This will lead to children graduating from high school and establish the foundation for their success. Therefore, this book serves as the field notes from diverse teaching experiences and the living languages of the field itself.

Contents

Chapter Ⅲ
Korean Culture to the World

Chapter Ⅳ
Sharing Different Culture

Chapter V
Living as a Minority

Chapter VI
Ka-mak-noon, A Modern-Day Illiterate

Chapter I

Education at Table

1.1 Developing Independence

At the restaurant I regularly visit, a few weeks ago, I ran across a girl who seemed to be a teenager. She was carrying a basket. I exclaimed when I peered inside.

"Oh! Your doll is so adorable!" "This is my baby, not a doll."

It was a very small, adorable, and pretty baby. So I mistook her for a doll. When I examined her closer, she was wiggling her little fingers and toes.

"She is tiny. How old is she?" I asked.
"She's a week old." she responded.

I was shocked and spoke to her.

"How could you bring a newborn baby to a public space like a restaurant?" "What if she gets infected by germs?" "It'll be easy for you, as a new mother, to get infected as well "

To my deep concerns, the girl, who looked quite like a student, replied,

"The doctor said it was fine."

I had heard that Western women went back to work a week or two after childbirth, but it was even more surprising to see it in person. In South Korea, newborns typically stay indoors until they are at least a hundred days old for their safety. New mothers also mostly stay inside for about three months, restraining from seeing many outsiders. In Korea and America, not only are the public perception and attention toward pregnant women but also the way of raising children are quite different.

A long time ago, toward the beginning of my time studying in the United State of America, I had a friend named Laura. She was a working woman with two children, and as was the case, I babysat for her at times. Every day, at one o'clock in the afternoon, she would put her children down for naps. They would be in the middle of playing, but when it was time, she would bring her children to the second floor and put them in their beds. The children, whose playtimes had been interrupted, would naturally cry. Laura would leave the crying children and come back downstairs. The babies' cries were so loud and uncomfortable that I still remember them clearly.

I thought it was quite cold and cruel. I felt that Westerners were so logical at times that I felt dispassionate. How could she leave her children to cry that much? I couldn't understand her at all at that time. It was a cultural shock to me. The children would cry for five or ten minutes, then go quiet. At times they would tire themselves out from crying and fall asleep, and other times, they would stay in their beds and play by themselves. Like this, it seemed like Western children learned of rules and independence from an early age.

When I was younger, I was taught that children cried for three reasons. As they could not speak, they would cry if they were hungry, hurting, or sleepy. Mothers would carry sleepy, crying babies on their backs or fall asleep next to them in bed. They never left the crying babies alone. I couldn't imagine leaving crying babies alone and waiting for them to fall asleep on their own. Like this, Korean mothers raised their children with intimacy, with skin-to-skin contact. There were even Korean fourth graders who did not leave their mothers' arms yet. Perhaps that is why we are more emotional and compassionate than others. It seems as though Western mothers are more logical.

<They key to child development, physical contact>

American psychologist Harry Harlow determined physical contact to be the most important part of children's development, claiming that it was a decisive factor in attachment formation. Physical touch made children feel intimate toward their mothers, enabling them to feel secure; feeding children or playing with them were surprisingly not as influential. For children, physical touch fosters stability, sensory development, confidence, and trust in others.

The research team at Baylor University School of Medicine found that children who received more physical touch were more intelligent; the proximity of the skin and the brain means that physical touch makes a big impact on children's brain development. The neural development of children who received more physical touch was 30% higher than children who did not. Furthermore, physical touch increases sociability; children are not as afraid of new environments or interpersonal relationships and acclimate to new situations faster. Children who received more physical contact have calmer dispositions and are more cheerful.

It would not be an overstatement to say that more physical contact, such as hugging, tickling, and play wrestling, brightens a child's future.

—Jul. 5, 2017

1.2 Teen Work Ethics

A young boy started working at age of 14 for the first time at a restaurant, helping chef in the kitchen. He wanted to buy a new motorcycle when he was a junior high school student. By law, he was not allowed to drive a car yet. Instead, he could ride motorcycle, allowed by law from age 14. He badly wanted to have his own transportation, a motorbike, so that he did not have to depend on his parents' ride or the school bus.

That summer, his parents promised him to buy a new motorbike as long as he worked a full time job for summer break. So his first job was washing and cleaning dishes at a restaurant kitchen. He had to wake up at 4 AM and assisted chefs to prepare for food at the restaurant. Teens need a lot of sleep and it's very hard for them to get up at 4AM. He, however, was happy to get up so early, thinking of having his own transportation and independent, feeling like a fine grown man.

All teens in South Korea have used public transportations; bus, train, or subway.

In American society, unlike Korea, there are few public buses and trains. Adolescents usually use parental transportation or school buses. So the American teenagers' dream is to have their own cars or motorbikes to be independent from their parents.

My husband in America and I in South Korea were born at almost same time and grew up in the same time period, but in the other side of the world, with very different environments: language, food, housing, and culture. He was raised in comfort in wealthy country, but I, in a very poor country, devastated by two wars, WWII and the Korean War. We have very interesting conversations, sharing our stories in the 1970s and 1980s. I am always very curious about his work experiences, American's work ethics, and employment in their teenage years.

Many American teens begin to learn very early a fundamental value that, without laboring, they cannot get what they want. American culture help teens educated that laboring is necessary for them to get what they want to have: It says that if you are alive, you have to work. Even if parents are very wealthy, their children still have to work to get what they want to have or do.

Regarding laboring and finance, if one needs money, he can borrow it without just taking it for granted and then pay it back later. One day, I was impressed when I saw that my husband paid back, as he promised his parents, even a small amount of borrowed money from them when he had an emergency. I always thought my parents' money was mine just like other Korean children did. I have seen only two times a year when my husband received a free money or gift from his parents;

birthday and Christmas. I learned that American parents' money is just parents' because they worked so hard; it does not belong to their children.

On the other hand, Korean teenagers make learning and studying a top priority and their greatest goals are to get admitted to prestigious top colleges. My parents also always asked me to only study hard without working any for money when I was in teen; in general, students only focus on learning and studying only when they are in high school.

When I needed money, my parents provided it until I graduated college and got a job. Even when the young Koreans got married, parents provided them money for wedding ceremony, for buying their furniture, and for buying house, including college tuition and their expenses. Until I graduated from college, I depended on my parents. My only labor was to babysit my younger sister and brothers and to help my parents with housework or errands.

My husband said that he was fine as long as he could get a grade of C or higher. His parents never pushed him nor gave him burden on GPA. He was satisfied when he received more than C grade without any school absences. Instead, He started to work every summer vacation and learned early the value of labor. So when Americans are high school students, they buy their own cars and gradually become independent mentally and physically from their parents. In the long run, I think that American boys and girls may be stronger and tougher in their crisis.

My husband and I were raised in very different environments; culture, foods, language. We had very different experiences, knowledge from the opposite sides of the earth. So it is very interesting for us to exchange our unique experiences and learned lots of things from each other. We also have to keep trying us to be balanced and to live in harmony everyday.

—Jul. 7, 2017

1.3 Homeroom Teacher as Counselor

One morning, an urgent call rang in our school. It was from the police in a neighboring city. The officer told the assistant principal that they were holding a student from my school and needed someone to pick him up. Any misbehavior of students in a school should be reported not only to the school principal but also to the student's homeroom teacher.

In a school, if a student is absent without any previous notice, it usually implies that something negative incidents happen. So principals, assistant principals, and homeroom teachers always, thoroughly check on the absent students every morning by 8-9AM. I used to give a call any student who did not show up on time in the morning.

By police report, during the previous weekend, a group of students stayed in a hotel. The hotel owner thought it was unusual and reported them to the police station because generally teens did not stay in a hotel by a teenage group without any adult. By the police investigation, one of these teens had stolen some money in a public bus. Then, he and his friends, including my student, spent the weekend, playing computer games and watching movies.

I was in my mid-20s and had just started teaching. So I was very embarrassed by the urgent police call and did not know exactly how to take care of the bad incident. My duty as a homeroom teacher was to resolve the case as soon as possible. I had to go to the police station to meet my student, praying that all would be fine. As soon as I saw him with the police, tears ran down my cheeks. He was from a very poor family and was neglected long time. So he had been hanging out with other students with problems.

My student had not stolen anything, but he had left home and stayed outside without telling his parents. This was a bad sign of future problems; he might do it again. He promised that he would not go out with those friends any more. He signed a statement that he would never do it again. I also signed that I would be responsible for his future behavior. This was the worst experience I ever had in my teaching career as a homeroom teacher. Fortunately, he graduated without any further incident since then.

Teenagers are so difficult to deal with not only in South Korea but also USA. When I came to the USA first, I stayed with an American family. A teen in the family had to stay at home and be homeschooled by his mother. He had been expelled from school for misbehavior in his classroom. Korean teachers would taken care of such teenagers' misbehaviors in school.

However, the school in USA have parents handle it at home. Fortunately, he finished his all assignments with strong support and great guidance from his parents and sister. He later graduated from high school and then college, got a good job, married, and then had two children. Now he is doing quite well.

Korean teachers have lots of responsibilities because schools have only a couple of school counselors, while there are lots of school counselors in American schools. They have a lot of other duties for students in career, college admissions, jobs, and personal issues as a counselor, inaddition their major duty, full time teaching. Half of the duty of Korean homeroom teachers have might be taken by counselors in American public schools. So one Korean family in USA might even say that if parents are not called by school counselors, they might believe that their children are doing fine in American public schools.

However, school counselors in America might be only able to care for the "official" problems of students. Their real, inside conflicts or problems are often ignored in school and at home. That is why dropout rate has been high in public high schools. In Korean public schools, though, homeroom teachers as counselors always spend a lot of time with their students from early morning from 7AM to late night, sometimes 10PM. So they are able to understand their students much better and can have much closer relationships with them.

Thus, Korean schools and parents with homeroom teachers' endless efforts and strong support from school community have had much fewer problems regarding lower dropout rate in public schools because schools could solve students' problems more easily, effectively with homeroom teachers as their counselor.

1.4 Everything at Dinner Table

My first year in the United States, I spent all my time studying, without really trying to adapt myself to my very new environment. After I had been here for a few years, though I had experienced a lot of American culture and had begun to understand the American system. I discovered some strikingly important factual statistics about the high school dropout rate as I was preparing for my dissertation. I found that the rate was very high, more than 50% in some urban school districts. I challenged myself to study this issue more deeply.

Governments collect a gigantic amount of tax from residents for local schools and to support free education from kindergarten to 12th grade; and for things such as school buildings, property, educational materials, school buses, teacher salaries, meals and soon. American students are very blessed compared to those in some other countries. Americans never imagine how much children in other countries envy and would love to have American resources for public schools.

Students in other countries might not understand why American students would disregard the resources available to them, and why they would even consider dropping out of school. Are they lazy, not caring about hard work or studying, as is sometimes thought? Do they have no pride, even though all these resources give them a great opportunity to study, get a job and live comfortably?

As I studied this issue, I began to understand such American students better, though. Some of them may have been raised with what might be described as a lack of confidence in failing. What do I mean by this? Korean children are trained and learn to have strong pride and self-esteem from their family and community. It means that they can adjust or adapt themselves to difficult conditions. Self-esteem makes them love and respect themselves. It gives them strong minds to meet challenges, and to try again even though they might have failed several times. Thus, they can change their lives in positive ways. High dropout rates indicate a lack of self-esteem and show that the students are failing to challenge themselves to overcome difficult situations.

For children, a positive social environment and family relationship promotes stronger self-esteem. Korean society requires that children respect their adults and keep pride in the community strong. In particular, education "at breakfast and dinner table" — that is, by parents and close relatives — is a tremendous influence on children's pride and will. In South Korea, children in the 1960s through the 1980s were raised under very high poverty levels after two wars, World War II and Korean War. But the "at table" education from parents and communities always emphasized high expectations of children based on a strong foundation of community relations and family. By contrast, American families in urban settings often have a weaker influence on this kind of lower educational expectation. This lack of family influence is correlated strongly with a high dropout rate. This cycle can repeat and worsen generation by generation. This is the assumption that I proved in my dissertation.

As an educator, I can see that strong monetary support and government assistance cannot end nor reduce these high school dropout rate or social problems. For the last few years, the Obama administration understood the causes of American school and social problems and made very unique solutions by providing early education, after school program, offering jobs for single mother and higher education support for minority families with single mothers in urban settings. His solutions were a type of education "at table" which compensated for a lack of parental involvement and discipline.

Some say the homeless in cities are very lazy. President Obama and educators saw these social and school problems differently, as a political systematic problem of minority groups that needed fixing in many different ways. I was not aware of the deep-rooted history of this political systematic problem of minorities until I started writing and researching my dissertation in graduate school, and after I had had some ten years' experience with American culture.

These systematically-abused minority groups in the past often lack the pride and self-esteem that might otherwise be gained from their families. Their children may never overcome their lack of pride; and pass along their low self-esteem generation to generation. Everyday parental lessons at home or education "at table" create a strong foundation of self-esteem in children, which can lead them to overcome any hardship in school or in society, and to a lifetime of success.

1.5 Bogging Down Young Boys

In South Korea, all public school teachers have to relocate to a different school every 5 or 6 years. After 6 years of teaching in an all-girls school, I was relocated to a boys' school. My first class of 40 students seemed very interested in studying English, with full of smiles on their faces. I was glad to see them because they seemed to be paying full attention to me. They followed every movement, smiling. I thought that these students loved learning English and how lucky I was to be in this school.

After class, one of the young female teachers whispered to me that the boys were getting ready to play a prank on me; they were going to hand around a mirror and try to see up my skirt. I kept my eyes open and caught some of boys trying it. I punished them, giving the heaviest punishment to the class president and class leaders.

At that time, most female teachers wore nice suits with skirts to be good female models for school community. In the boys' school, I was surprised to see that female teachers wore pants or even jeans. I came to understand later that teen boys are very mentally and physically different from teen girls, and I realized that teachers had to teach and educate them very differently from girls.

Teen boys may look grown physically but their mental status is still very immature. Sometimes, I think that boys' minds are full of nothing but sex. They are interested in all kinds of sexual stuff, from putting mirrors under skirts to pretending to fall down in the hallway to see up teachers' or girls' skirts. We found all kinds of foreign adult magazines in their book bags. I learned in the boys' school that a teen boy's biggest interest is in sex.

Regarding the teen boys' special characters, however I was so concerned on bogging down young boys. Recently, CNN reporter Lisa Ling investigated and broadcast a special report on teen sex crimes. She noted the case of a naive teenage boy who went to a party at a friend's house with a group of other teen boys. A group of girls was there and one girl sat on his lap. He was embarrassed by this, but let her sit on his knee. Later, the girl reported to police that she had been raped and sexually assaulted. The boy was arrested based upon her accusation.

A lawyer persuaded him to confess that he had done the crime, telling him that the police would let him go back home. So, even though he didn't want to, he confessed to the rape. Far from being allowed to go home, however, he was put on trial and sent to prison for 10 years and then had to register as a sex offender. Ling mentioned that many other teen boys, because of similar small mistakes, now live in a kind of hell. Simple teenage curiosity and immaturity leads to long prison sentences for some.

These days college campuses are also often the sites of sexual assault cases. A report by Fox News' John Stossel recommended a boy almost seems to have to get a contract signed by a girl before they could date. Immature boys have a strong curiosity regarding sex and are very vulnerable to intrigue from girls. Sometimes false accusations of sexual assault often can be in issue. Boys are often unaware of this type of dangerous swamp, bogging down them for long time. They may not realize how much serious trouble they would be in.

I was raised listening to adults who said "Be careful of any man." Now I would say to teen boys, "Be careful of sexy girls, who can make you sink into a swamp forever."

1.6 My Dad's Christmas

At the Christmas party in my parents in law's house, I first discovered exotic foods that I had never tasted before on the dinner table, along with colorful beautiful decorations. Pretty candles, beautiful flowers, and decorations made the table unique and elegant. We all had a wonderful time with delicious food and delightful stories. We started opening the gifts that had been gathered around the Christmas tree as the Christmas party surged on. The Christmas party was lots of fun, with excited kids running and jumping and dogs running after them, wagging their tails.

Gift-exchange time lasted a couple of hours. Most of the gifts were for the little children but there were some for the adults, too. We exchanged gifts, greetings, blessings, and good wishes followed. We took pictures and laughed during this pleasant time. Sometimes, a prank was going on too. For example, a child tried to open a 60 inch high box, out of which sprang his uncle, making the child squeal with mixed terror and delight. We all laughed at the scene.

Preparing and opening special gifts for family can make us more closely connected and reconfirm the ties of family relationships. Preparing a gift for family is an expression of care and love. Parties with wonderful food, events, fun stories and games, help bring families closer together. It is the biggest festival of the year. However, most Americans celebrate Christmas as the anniversary of Jesus' birth, but all are not particularly pious Christians.

On our way home after the annual Christmas party, I was thinking about the Christmases of my youth in South Korea. When I was a little girl, I was taught to behave in a very restrained manner on Christmas Day, because my dad, as a pastor, used to tell us that Jesus had been born in a shabby, wretched stable, and was laid in a manger, so we should not enjoy Christmas in luxurious and wealthy way either. We should be quiet, humble, restrained, and devout, and not focus on materialism. Thus, we spent Christmas quietly, calmly, humbly, and devoutly.

When I think about my life in 1960s-70s Korea, I remember that we lived in great political conflict and economically-poor period after World War II and Korean War. It might have been necessary for us to live in a humble and pious way. In addition, at that time, Korean society was against Christianity, instead emphasizing Buddhism and traditional Korean religion, called YouKyo. Christianity did not follow our culture and social ethics such as ancestor-worship. My dad had to fight mentally, against non-Christians as a pioneering Christian pastor. My father's congregation were also criticized by his own family members and other non-Christians.

As a result, my Christmases were more simple and humble. As I grew up, I experienced and began to accept the changes in the nature and meaning of Christmas; it became more for commercial profit and secular events. But when I met my American husband, my idea of Christmas changed again. It became a time of happiness and fun with family. As soon as Thanksgiving is over, Americans begin preparing for Christmas events. But sometimes, though, I feel like something is missing. I think about those old Christmases, and the commercialization that has become part of our modern festivities, and I think that maybe it would be better if our modern celebrations were somewhere between my father's and my husband's Christmases.

— Dec. 25, 2015

1.7 Individualism vs. Community Power

Other countries might envy the most the US public library system. Most cities have a pubic library. Any information or news about the local town can be found in the library. The library prepares fully for the different need of residents; Students find references, parents with young children enjoy participating in reading programs, seniors can read large-print books, and there may even be English classes for foreigners trying to learn English.

I often visited a public library in my town. One morning, around 10:00AM, I saw three teens at a computer station in the library computer lab who were playing computer games. I had a habit from my teaching profession that made me look at students closely when I saw them as if I was still a teacher in charge of discipline. I asked them a couple of questions with full of curiosity.

"You are middle school students, aren't you?"

"Yes."

"It is 10AM now. You should be in school instead of playing computer games here in the public library."

"……" They did not answer me.

I sharply told them, as a professional habit and out of a feeling of responsibility to our community. "You guys, if you do not go to school right now, I will call the middle school principal and tell him what you are doing now."

As soon as I said this, they picked up their book bags, rushed out of the lab, and ran to the B school gate direction.

Later, I told my husband what I had done at the library. He advised me, "Americans do not interfere with other people's business even when they are doing something wrong." "It is not a good idea to meddle in others' business."

Americans value first and foremost, individual opinions and each person's rights to liberty and individualism. I told him, "it maybe other's business but at the end, it affects our community, which we are responsible for. Therefore, it is my job." For example, students drop-outs make our society more vulnerable to problems.

In order to prevent students from being absent or drop-outs, In South Korea, by 8-10AM, most k-12 schools have already checked attendance, listed the names on the teacher's room board, and are aware any absentees. Homeroom teachers are very nervous about their students being absent. They receive an extra stipend as a homeroom teacher due to the extra responsibility for the homeroom class students like as counselors in the United States. While they have a busy schedule, teaching, counseling, and doing administrative work, they make phone calls to the absentees and find out the reasons why they are absent before reporting absentees to the school principal. Korean schools thoroughly prepare and plan to avoid any bad incidents.

On the other hand, American schools are different from Korean ones. American public schools do not have the same strong homeroom teacher system to check every students' school life. In US public schools, counselors rather than teachers, take care of major student problems. I believe that it is not as effective as homeroom teacher system does in Korea, to resolve students' conflicts. That is why other authorities, like security guards or police officers, are on duty in school in the United States.

I guess that teens do not communicate with counselors deeply on their sensitive issues except for official matters. They often do not discuss personal problems and talk about personal conflicts with, except their friends. That is one reason why more students drop-outs happen.

Individualism results in a less healthy society in my opinion and can lead to more relieve on the welfare system. It leads to higher taxes and tremendous spending by more government agencies. Thus, I would say that these problems become our responsibility in the end. We need community responsibility, not just individualism; each of us should take ownership. Counselors, teachers, and police can NOT take care of all the problems of our school communities.

In an ideal society we respect individual rights, individualism and liberty, but making a healthy, better society should also be our goal. Local schools need our ownership and stronger community responsibility, community power.

— Feb. 23, 2017

1.8 My Destiny; My Better Half

At the beginning of my studies in USA, I used to ask for the help of the campus police whenever I was in a potentially dangerous or difficult situation at night. This time, I also tried to call the campus police. I could not get my car out of the parking lot because it was locked up due to construction. It was already dark and hard to see anything. I found a public telephone booth near my car and tried to call for help to get my car out of the locked parking lot.

As I was dialing 911, a young man behind me spoke to me.
"May I help you? You look like you are having trouble."
I knew him from the Research Methodology class, and we had spoken several times before in other places, computer lab and library.

I refused his help because I was used to asking campus police for help, and they always responded me quickly and helped nicely.
"I do not need your help. Do not worry about me."
"If I call the campus police for help, they come out here right away."
He, however, took my phone and talked to school police to help me.
"Don't be afraid of me. I am here to help you."

Then he took the phone away from my hand and spoke to the police for me. He thought he needed to help me because I was a foreigner with broken English and was unfamiliar with American life. He thought I was in danger because it was so dark outside around 9PM. He finished talking to the campus police on the phone and explained me that the parking lot would be reopened the next morning at 7am.

I had an important morning appointment the next day and I was worried about the meeting. He offered to drive me to my apartment that night and to the meeting the next day. I was not comfortable with his offer at all but I took it. He drove me to my apartment, about 15 minutes away. Amazingly, early the next morning, around 6:45AM, he came to my apartment and drove me to my car.

I had originally met this guy at the computer lab in the College of Education. He asked me several questions. I responded with very quick and short answers and then left there quickly. At that time I was interested only in my future career and studying in the USA. Then, I met him again in my Child Development Psychology class but did not communicate with him. He always sat in the first or second row in class and paid full attention to instructor or actively participated in discussions. Thus, he made a good impression on the instructor. I was always sitting quietly in the back row.

I warmed up to him after the parking lot locked incident with my car. He also seemed to feel that my attitude had changed toward him. So he often stopped me in college library and asked if I was interested in

My half color

having lunch with him. I usually accepted because I wanted to learn more about traditional Southern American culture and social issues. I sometimes spent time with him on the weekends and we became casual friends.

I became comfortable talking with him. Unlike many young Korean men, he never pretended to be drunk or to move too fast. He never tried to get uncomfortably closer to me than necessary, and never tried to hold my hand secretly or leaned on me. He really made me comfortable and never pushed me away by disclosing his sexual emotions toward me. I was not ready to date anybody and he accepted my non-romantic attitude and kept waiting for me, very nicely, like an English noble gentleman. He never came on strong or pushed me when I was not ready for any romantic relationship. I had never seen a man like him with such good manners and a great patience. I could hang around with him without any problem. I did not have to run away from him.

Later, I came to understand the values and attitudes of Westerners in relationships, learning more Western culture and lifestyles. It seems to me that Westerners are aware of sexual assault laws and very cautious when dating.

He was very careful, not trying to touch me, nor even my clothes. I became very comfortable with him, began to see his positive side, and gradually became more accepting of him .

It is very important for Korean men to wait until a lady is ready for a relationship. But it is hard for Korean men to wait such a long time; even one year. In the United States, Americans are accustomed to being cautious and waiting until a lady is ready for a relationship. In Korea, there are many sexual assault victims who do not openly discuss their assaults in public. Even when the crimes are reported, the women are often victimized again by the public. So women are very cautious around men.

After spending a lot of time with this guy, however, it happened to have him as my destiny, my better half. I never imagined before, even for a second, that I would have American husband because I planned to go back to South Korea and to work for a university or government.

Chapter II

Korean Community in Atlanta, GA

2.1 A Statue of Peace for Comfort Women

Installing a comfort women statue in Atlanta has been difficult, disturbed by Japanese political leaders. Korean leaders however finally was able to install it in a park, near downtown Atlanta. I tried to attend at the ceremony event.

It was so hard to locate a special statue. With an exact address and additional instructions in details, I was finally able to find the event place with the statue of a peace for comfort women. It was in a small space next to a senior apartment complex in Decalb county. The space is called Blackburn 2 Park. It is in between a senior apartment complex and town houses. I felt that the girl statue for comfort women was abandoned in a lonely isolated corner in a strange foreign country far from our home country. Japanese authority has been strongly against building the statue in Atlanta, GA.

It was hard to walk through the muddy garden by heavy rain and muddy soil. The garden was like a swamp. I barely walked through toward the statue. A white metal sign beside the statue was seen first as I approached it. The white metal sign was wrongly indicated that the memorial was intended to bring attention to the problem of sex trafficking in Atlanta. Atlanta is a top city in the sex trafficking in US. It is shameful and this girl's statue was promoting the alert of the sex trafficking and the criminal activities.

"Well, the sign does not describe any of historic facts of Japanese cruelty toward Korean girls in World War II."

After listening to my comment, Anthony who was taking down the pavilion at the end of the event started reading the controversial white sign closely and said,

"It is a warning of sex trafficking in Atlanta which is a top city in USA."

He agreed that whoever read this sign would think of that this statue only means the warning of sex trafficking.

"This girl's statue of peace is not that simple meaning. Japanese invaded South Korea in WWII. Japan colonialized South Korea for 36 years. We could not use our language Korean, all young and healthy Korean men were drafted and had to fight for Japan. Girls were forced to comfort soldiers in WWII. The original purpose of the statue intended that we should remember the Japan's cruelty in the war."

Anthony seemed so perplexed by listening my explanation. And then he looked down a black square stone underneath the girl's statue and read through thoroughly the engraved letters on the stone, wiping out the rainy water. Then he said,

"The stone describes every small part of Korean history on WWII that you just mentioned. It is not enough but more explicit the white sign."
"I would have known that the girl's statue meant only a sex trafficking if you had not explained me in detail about the special historic meaning of the statue. Thank you for your special addition for me !"

I explained more about Japanese invasion and some their cruelties across the North Eastern Asia during WWII.

"Wow, it is so surprising that this girl's statue is related to such important Korean historic issues !"
"Most people would not know the statue's meaning if they read only

the white sign noticeable easily to anybody."

Anthony added that every country seemed to have such a sad history of political, systematic power, leaving many institutional victims behind, his face darkened because the girl's statue recalled the sacrificed past, as a black man, of a sad history of his grand, great parents and ancestors in USA.

In the evening I read an English newspaper article on building the girl's statue. The article and some comments on the news was unbelievable: Japanese consulate was saying that comfort women were voluntary prostitutes". All Koreans, of course, think that his shameless remark was very absurd, though. Some comments were so logical, coherent and hard to be against persuasively without comprehensive knowledge on Korean history and understanding Korean culture. It looked like that Americans who did not have any background knowledge could believe easily the news article and its long distorted comments.

Young Koreans are good at English but do not know the detailed historical facts well. Older Koreans know Korean history and culture better than the young, but English is not fluent enough to refute English comments and most of them are confined to everyday life, and do not have any passion nor time for the issues. For these reasons, the elaborate and logical excuses and distortions of Japanese history on WWII continue. I felt so burden to think about the long journey that our next generation should fight against the distorted history made by Japan.

In the evening my American husband also mentioned about the statue because local media was noisy about building a Korean girl's statue in Atlanta, GA.

"Building a Korean girl's statue for comfort women of WWII is so controversial, isn't it ?"

I was very surprised by his comment.

"It's an one-sided, distorted history created by Japan. They might not like to accept their own faults made by their ancestors. They harassed our ancestors by invading our country for 36 years. I grew up listening all the time to directly our grand parents about the atrocities of Japan when I was young."

"Oh yeah? 36 years?"

My husband also reminded his memories when he was young.

"Actually, when I was a kid, an old man who was living next door, was drafted to World War II. He hated Japan very much. Most Americans, however, thought that they should be able to live first and get economically better than following his witnesses, and prioritizing their dealings with Japan. And after World War II folks died, almost all Americans forget or do not know about Japanese atrocities.
Over the years, the history of the war has largely disappeared from Americans' memories."

Listening to my husband's story, I hope that our next generation is able to study history more deeply with passion to correct the distorted history of WWII made by Japan. I hope that both governments and corporations are able to work together to inform the truth of the Second World War created by Japan, as has been shown in the process of building the girl's statue in Blackburn with several Korean and American civilians.

Addition : After a controversy over the installation site, two months later, September 9, the girl's peace statue was moved and settled into Blackburn Main Park, which is larger and more prospective.

2.2 437,000(Four Hundred Thirty Seven Thousand)

The number of 437,000 is not the amount of money nor the number of lottery ticket. It is the mileage displayed on the automobile dashboard of Kia Sedona made by Korean Kia company. The car is 10 years old car. The car with such a high mileage is seen first. Kia Sedona is particularly useful when transporting relatively large items such as beds or sofas and it is a van, like a large SUV style.

Since the 1980s, I have often heard that the Kia Motors are built very well. At that time, many young Kia Motors researchers were sent to Germany to study the excellence of German automobiles. This remarkable sign of excellence, extreme high mileage, which I have confirmed with my own eyes today, is the number of commercial vehicles driven everyday by a gentleman who run a barbecue restaurant in Alabama Montgomery. He still boasts that it runs smoothly at speeds of over 90 mph.

In the 1980s and '90s in Korea, many people, including me, used to buy a new car every 5 years when buying a domestic car. Most domestic used cars were exported to China, where demand for automobiles was so high at the time. Used cars were hard to find at that time. On the other hand, in the 1990s, young people in the United States used old Japanese cars due to economic matter and long mileage. The Japanese cars were very popular at that time because of their excellent performance.

When I first came to the United States in 1997, I also bought a 10-year-old Toyota Camry with 85,000 miles on it, for only $3000.00 from an international student. The performance of the 1986 Camry was so fantastic that I became a Toyota maniac from then on. I still cannot forget the pleasant sense of driving the Camry, which ran smoothly, quietly, and steadily even at high speeds, something I had never felt with a Korean car. A few years later, when the Camry reached 145,000 miles, it was great to be able to sell it to a used car dealer for $1,500.

The degree to which Japan contributed to the US economy in 1970s-2000s was often not recognized by US residents. Many Americans, including acquaintances and relatives I know, worked at many Japanese companies, especially car manufacturers.

As an example of the influence of Japanese on the economy of GA, when I met a local school superintendent in the 1999, he immediately assumed that, as an Asian in GA, I was Japanese. the back of his business card that the superintendent handed was filled with Japanese. He greeted me very kindly with Japanese and guided and helped me like he treated me his best customer. He misunderstood me as a

Japanese. It was a pleasure to see that Japan had created a positive image of East Asia, but at the same time I felt sad that Korea did not have the same status.

However, in the 21st century, products produced in South Korea, like the Kia Sedona, can be seen in many ways to perform better than Japanese ones. Many Japanese companies that had flourished have closed their doors while Korean products are now found in many American classrooms and homes: TVs, cars, Android cell phones and so on. Korean economic and power is getting stronger.

A friend of mine, who immigrated from Korea forty years ago told me that when he had used American cars, he had to fix them so often that his knowledge about automobiles had increased. Since 1994, he has been using only Hyundai cars and he has not had any problem with them. He has driven the Hyundai Sonata almost 200,000 miles, but it's still running well. In addition to the sophisticated appearance and the comfort and user friendliness of their interiors, Korean cars have improved their performance and quality to a world class level.

Georgia State Governor Nathan Deal in recognition of the excellent quality and performance of Korean cars, officially announced that Kia Motors would produce Georgia State's official vehicles. An American I know, who used to love Toyota and Honda, like me, tried to buy a Kia car recently. However, he had to wait for several months to receive the model he wanted to buy because Kia cars have become so popular. Hyundai and Kia seem to have become the best cars in America soon.

2.3 Business, The Most Trusted and Reliable

There is a car repair shop that I regularly visit. The owner doesn't speak much, and is not as handsome as an actor. He does not often smile. He just works as hard as he can. He inspects my ten-year old car and does not advise me to fix it unless it is in a really dangerous condition. If someone compares his service with others, he would know that he only charges half the regular price. His customers are almost always regular visitors to the shop.

A foreign woman who visits today is one of the customers who visit regularly even though she drives a long distance to see him, as I do. There are many visitors like me who have used this service station for over 20 years. Not only women who don't have any basic knowledge to take care of their cars, but also people who know about cars give him their business, because they trust him to take care of their cars with good, high quality service at a minimal cost. I have come to think of him as a beautiful person. Twenty-two years after I first started going to him, he still cares for my troublesome car with honesty and forthrightness.

The first time I met him was in 1997 when I first came to study in the United States. I drove a 10-year-old Toyota Camry. When everything in USA was new and unfamiliar to me, my car broke down. Many other mechanics made me embarrassed because they said, "Buy another car" or "You might spend more money fixing this car than buying a new one." But he repaired only the damaged parts of my car and told me not to worry about cosmetic part of damage, as long as the car was safe. I paid only a tenth of what others tried to charge me. After a few years, my car ran smoothly without any problems.

The business owner counseled and helped all his guests equally, respecting everyone equal. Even during the recession, when many other businesses in the US shut down, his business in Doraville was doing well because regular customers kept coming, keeping him busy. His spirit seems to be even more beautiful because many other business owners cheat their customers, charging double or triple, for example. It is hard for me to find such a dependable business owner. There have been several fraud cases reported in the auto service area, cooperating with insurance companies.

In other business field, for example, there are many restaurants across country. workers in restaurants work hard to live, but the restaurant owners often live luxuriously. They donate to welfare organizations to help the poor and promote their businesses with a good image and receive tax benefits, while making their employees work for minimum wage. They are catching two rabbits. There is a lot of this kind of imbalance in our society. Many businesses do not help their workers enough while making themselves look good by donating to charities and welfare organizations.

When oil price began to rise in the mid 2000s, up, the cost of a barrel of crude increased by more than $100 per barrel. This led to an increase in the price of fuel. Airlines decided to raise their prices for this reason. Recently, crude oil prices have fallen to less than half what they were, but airfares have not gone down. Many passengers complain but are ignored by power of Airline leaders.

Five years ago, I joined the Connecting Business and Market Place to Christ (CBMC), an international community that communicates the gospel to businessmen and professionals. Christianity and business may seem to be antithetical to each other so I wondered how businessmen live as true Christians, unlike other average business owners. I had a strong curiosity about this meeting in terms of the love of Jesus giving up himself and the act of getting profit out of others. The conclusion is that CBMC members are better than those who do not believe in Jesus because the group members at least try to live biblically. Chic-fil-A corporation is based on biblically originated business, first created in Atlanta, GA.

The Chic-fil-A corporation is a chain of popular American chicken sandwich restaurants. Every morning, many Americans sit in long lines at the Chick-fil-A drive-through to get their breakfasts. The company president lives in our neighborhood and sometimes I can see him driving on the street. Generally, restaurants in the USA are so crowded that business owners never close on Sundays. It is sometimes said that restaurants can live a week on their Sunday income. I used to wait in long line with my husband at restaurants after worship every Sunday.

However, all Chick-fil-A restaurants are closed on Sundays, specifically to allow their employees a day for family and worship, but their business has grown very rapidly, and it is now one of top companies in GA because of their honesty, respect, and strong faith.

It was very hard for me to adapt myself on such long waiting lines at first. Even worse, Sunday is much more expensive than other days. There are many restaurants that open their doors on Sundays and live without much business on weekdays, because they charge more on Sundays. However, Chick-fil-A restaurants, which close on Sundays, are doing very well; often much better than others. The restaurant distinguishes itself from other companies by its cleanliness, minimum profit, and the best service.

The beautiful people like my mechanic or the president of Chick-fil-A can make a difference with honesty and respect. Our society can be a better place when those with humble, good attitudes listen to their customers and respect and care for them truly.

— *Mar. 23, 2016*

2.4 Backbone, Korean Church Community, to Immigrants

Pastor Chung's death was so sudden that I could not believe it at first. I heard of his death on Facebook soon after he passed away in the hospital. He seemed so healthy that the news of his death did not seem real. Pastor Chung's leadership has had a powerful unifying effect on the Korean Christians community in Atlanta and around the world. He delivered good news to the Atlanta Korean community almost every day. He also helped many Korean immigrants overcome obstacles in their lives, and made their faith stronger. In recent years, some large Korean churches have had conflicts due to various incidents, but this rarely happened in Pastor Chung's church.

Pastors in immigrant churches have a different role than pastors in South Korea. Korean churches in the Korean immigrant community in the United States form a unique culture that is very different from that of local American churches. Korean churches are, naturally, deeply rooted in Korean immigrant culture and society. This is evident in the role of Korean immigrant churches in the language issues facing Korean immigrants.

The structure of the Korean language, or Hangul, is as unique as the Korean traditional religion YouKyo, which prioritizes the value of family and ancestral traditions. It is very different from the structure of the English language, even more different than the structure of Japanese or Chinese, so it is difficult for Koreans to learn English compared to other Asian immigrants. Many Koreans who immigrated after the Korean War had great difficulty adapting to American culture and society because of the language barrier. These immigrants often found help with such problems in Korean churches, strengthening their faith and joining a familiar community at the same time.

For example, a Korean old woman I know, who immigrated to the United States after the Korean War, was married to an American man. One day, early in her marriage, she and her husband had an argument, and she wanted to express her feelings to him, but she did not know the right words in English. Some of her friends at church, who were fluent in English, helped her to put her feelings into words, and she was able to tell her husband what she wanted to say in English.

When I listened to her life story in USA, I realized that her current comfortable life did not just happen one day – she worked hard to achieve it. I also learned how important the immigrant church was to Korean immigrants in the 1950s through the 2010s. Immigrant churches and their pastors have formed wonderful communities, helping them solve their problems. Even now, immigrant churches are places where immigrants who are struggling with language or culture can go and seek help from Korean pastors and congregations. Many immigrants also feel comfortable asking their pastors for help because they believe the pastors to be more than ordinary people. Pastors live (or should live) biblically-correct lives and be examples to others in the Korean community. Just as Pastor Chung was, a good pastor is a good Christian role model, and a good servant to his community.

I know a Korean family who received lots of helps from a church when they first moved to Atlanta, GA. They wanted their children to study in the US public school system. Although they did not speak English well, their children were still able to register and go to school. The parents could not speak English well either, and their Korean pastor at a church helped their children with problems and conflicts that happened in the school. The members of Korean churches and their pastors often take care of immigrant families who are not accustomed to American language and culture. It is an extension of the traditional tenets of Korean society and religion, which emphasize family, community values, and the traditions of our ancestors.

Korean churches and pastors listen to the voices of Korean immigrants and help to take care of the various issues they face. Korean immigrant churches often become surrogate families for immigrants. Success in Korean immigrant society is often due to be very direct and indirect assistance from churches and pastors. I would like to thank these pastors for their hard work, remembering the words of Pastor Chung In-Soo: "Church members have the right to misunderstand pastors, but the pastors have no opportunity to make excuses." I am grateful that the church community and its leaders are energetic sources of help and support for hard-working and often lonely Korean immigrants. I believe that Pastor Chung is in eternal peace in heaven.

— *May 17, 2016*

2.5 The Invisible, Outstanding Leader

I have a friend at Emory University in Atlanta whom people there call "Dr. Emory." He is wise and so knowledgeable that he can resolve almost any problem. He is the best technician in the facility management department at Emory. However, the prestigious private university also seems to have a somewhat prejudiced side when it comes to fair personnel management. He has been passed over four times for promotional opportunities. However, because he is a well-mannered and traditionally-minded Korean, with the ethics inherited from Confucian tradition, he never complained. If this kind of thing had happened to someone of a different (nonwhite) ethnicity, it would likely have been seen as racial discrimination, and the university might stand to lose millions of dollars in a lawsuit.

The first time I met this man was at a Catholic Church meeting. He was doing a lot of work as a Catholic leader. He and his family moved to Atlanta in the early 1980s, so he is witness to the long history of the Atlanta Korean community. As an engineer he participated in the early urban planning process of Peachtree City, south of Atlanta where I have lived for decades. He graduated from the most prestigious high school in South Korea, and majored in engineering in college, then moved to the US with his wife. After a failed attempt at starting his own business, he obtained US engineering certification and started working at Emory University. He loves Emory and is glad to be a part of the University.

He is also a patriot, which he shows in his actions, not just his words. He has helped Korean immigrants with many issues from the beginning of his time in the US. He values Korean companies and only Hyundai cars. He is proud of informing people that Korean cars are excellent and convenient. He also has a role as a diplomat. He was one of founding members of the Korean American Association of Atlanta, in the early 1980s, when Koreans were rare in the city. He does what is right and quietly works hard to spread traditional Korean values in American society.

Emory should reconsider him for promotion because he has more than the necessary qualifications. He is a husband and the father of three sons, and he takes good care of his family. He is a model for young people in the Atlanta Korean community. His sons, inspired by their father's service to the Korean community, have devoted themselves to helping their community in the medical field.

He speaks English very well, unlike some other immigrants. He has a good sense of humor and enjoys making his colleagues laugh. He enjoys working and helping his colleagues. He is diligent and is the first person to arrive at work each day. He checks his work schedule thoroughly every morning and does his best to make the Emory family comfortable. He always thinks positively and works hard.

One day he received a leg injury vacation which might have kept himself out of work for weeks. But he returned to work very quickly. His long-used campus vehicle was passed on to another person, and he had to walk every day around the large campus. Although he was in pain at first, he kept walking these long distances uncomplainingly, overcoming the pain from his injury. He was even thankful for walking every day – he says it helped him recover more quickly. He shows a true positive attitude for Korean young people, since he has the power to turn negative situations into positive.

He also has broad engineering knowledge and technology skills. He received perfect scores on the knowledge tests he had to take during the promotion process, but even this did not help him to have a chance to promote his job position. Emory University is fortunate to have such a wonderful person who works so loyally. The omission of his name from the promotion lists does not make sense at all – in fact it is downright unreasonable.

He is not alone, though. There are many such Korean patriots in North America. They work very hard, but never get the spotlight. I am very proud of these patriots who struggle in silence. They reflect the unique traditions of the Korean Confucian spirit and cultural heritage.

I however believe that Korean community and organizations or leaders may need to reevaluate the position of working Koreans in American Society. It is wonderful to be the kind of person like Jung with Korean virtue: kind, diligent, and uncomplaining. But this is not Korea. Social attitude and culture in US are a little different. I think that the the Korean virtue, traditional mind set, is not working well with unreasonable people. We need to stand up ourselves. We deserve it in the promotion. We should do everything we can to get what we deserve in the United States of America.

— Aug. 24, 2016

2.6 Air Show, A Remember of Korean War

There is a small airfield in the little town where I live. Every year this airfield puts an air show, one of the highlights in the area. Many visitors purchase the air show tickets every year and come to see this small town. However, a few weeks before the air show, many pilots practice flying for the show, and sometimes I feel very uncomfortable because loud noises from the planes seem to pierce my eardrum. Residents in the town seem to no longer care about the show because it has been an annual event for long time.

A few years ago, the airfield started offering a new flight training program and residents more often heard plane noise from the practice-flights. Sometimes they made too much noise and produced a bad smell like gunpowder which hurt my head. Often they do not respect the minimum altitude limit and I feel like they are just above the roof of my house. It reminds of my childhood experiences in South Korea.

In the 1970s, when I was a little girl, many air shows were held on the banks of the river in front of my small countryside hometown even though the Korean War had been over for a decade or so. I heard stories of the War from my family, neighbors, and teachers. So I felt that young Western soldiers, who were different from us, seemed like our saviors, and that their armored cars and air shows were dependable and trustworthy to me. In those days, we often felt a high level of tension in South Korea; quite often we met soldiers who were in training on land or conducting military exercises in airplanes.

I often waved to soldiers as they passed through my town with armored vehicles and saw airplanes flying overhead, along with the very irritable noise made by the military exercises. In the aftermath of the Korean War, South Korea was in a state of total emergency preparation for another possible attack by North Korea. There was a general consensus that Koreans would no longer be defenseless in another North Korean invasion.

Our society has always been prepared for another possible North Korean invasion since the Korean War. For example, we started civil defense education and training in the general public, anti-communism education among k-12 curriculum, and simulated war training as part of Korean military. Girls in high schools also required 'military-like drills' course as an extension of this social and political atmosphere. The course was to provide all Korean girls with both military training and nursing education as a part of the emergency preparedness.

According to Korean soldiers' testimonies, they, including my father, had to fight against the North Korean soldiers, on the last front line in 1950, to keep the last part of South Korea, Busan, and its surrounding small towns, near our neighborhood. Soldiers put themselves into a bloody battle to protect Busan, the last piece of land in South Korea. The battle of Yeongcheon Hyeongsan River, neighboring our hometown, was such a battlefield of death once they were deployed there. Many soldiers fought in the battlefield after only a week of training. Many

My father, a Korean War veteran

of the young people were killed or wounded on the battlefield.

The wounded had to live with the scars of war for the rest of their lives. My father was shot by the North Korean army, but he was saved by the emergency medical team and was able to meet my family again. So, the Western soldiers, who were aliens to Koreans, were recognized as saviors to me. They helped our troops, who had been pushed to the last line near Busan, retook our capital, Seoul, and then took even all parts of North Korea, putting the flags of South Korea and UN on the top of BaegDu Mountain, the boarder of China and North Korea, until the Chinese armies entered North Korea and did the battle line get pushed south to its present location.

The two wars, World War II and the Korean War, caused South Korea to become so impoverished that Koreans' lives could not be adequately expressed in words; they did not have enough to eat nor wear, and received various aids from the West. In particular, American Christian missionaries played a major, large role in aiding South Korea. They helped Christianity spread easily and widely across South Korea, which helped Koreans were opened-minded to Western and foreign culture. My father used to adhere to our traditional religion, Confucian Buddhism, also started a new habit of reading the Bible every day, and eventually he became a pastor, helping the needy, and spreading Christianity in my town.

My mother used to say that she had never dreamed that Koreans' wealthy lives would have happened in the 21st century. She felt that a miracle happened in South Korea because after the two wars, there had been no hope at all. Recently South Korea often helps other countries. This happened in only 40 years after the Korean War. We are helping starving people on the other side of the world, personally and nationally.

I also frequently see Korean leaders deliver donations and appreciation plaques to Korean War veterans in the United States. Recently, there was a ceremony to give scholarships to the grandchildren of Korean War veterans. These veterans, now in their 80s and 90s, were soldiers in the Korean War. I was so impressed and moved when I met the veterans who were holding their grandchildren's hands and receiving the scholarships from Atlanta Korean leaders.

I have mixed feelings with the current air show in this little town. The air show taking place in the sky now would be just a 'show' for fun sightseeing but unfortunately bring my sad memory of Korean war history into this peace place a little town.

— *Jun. 10, 2016*

Korean National Cemetary

2.7 Good Place for the Blind

Living in the United States is embarrassing when you have problems with your car. No car, no feet. One day I had a problem with my car and I asked my neighbor to drive me to where I needed to be. The neighbor waited for me in front of my house. In her back seat, a young, beautiful woman sat beside a Labrador Retriever. She had been a nurse for more than ten years. Her eyesight worsened and she eventually became blind, depending on her dog's help. She has been trying to overcome the obstacles with the help of her family, friends, and neighbors. She said that she would work for the blind for the rest of her life. My neighbor also gives her a ride whenever she needs one.

One of my colleague, who is in her forties, has suffered a great deal because of her blindness. She is trying to overcome the obstacle with the help of her family. How terrible she has been feeling when she became a blind. I was perplexed by even a little car problem, especially in the United States. I tried to find a service facility for her because she does not speak English well. It was very hard to find a service facility for a blinded Korean woman.

During a trip to Seoul last summer, I used public transportation, buses and subways, instead of taxis or cars. I thought that using buses or subways would be fun. One morning I walked down a street to catch the bus and waited for a green traffic signal to cross the crosswalk. I saw a bell on the pole next to the traffic light. There were braille points(the raised letters) on the bell for the blind. I was even more impressed to hear a guide voice saying there was a HyoJa-dong crossing. When I pushed on the bell, the voice provided additional information. I was so moved by the remarkable improvement and changes in South Korea for the people with disabilities.

At that time, a blind person walked diligently toward his destination in the morning. Even in the crowd, the dignified and relaxed figure was stood out. He might be the federal government official I met a few days ago. Thirty years ago, in the 1980s, Special education, institutions, and welfare facilities for the disabled were so undeveloped. We were urged to learn policies, educational systems, institutions, and welfare facilities for the disabled from the developed country such as the United States, EU, and Japan.

Now the public transportation system is well built everywhere in South Korea. Subways and buses are easily accessible to the public. The information guide system is electronic and the movements of all the city buses are shown on the board of each bus station in real time. The disabled, blind, or deaf are guided and receive the audiovisual assistance before the buses arrive. Now, it seems that the blind and deaf are adapting themselves well as members of our society.

But there are also many people who lost both their hearing and sight. Many of them stay in the multiple handicapped facilities operated by my acquaintances. Those who are deaf, blind, and unable to speak are still trying to overcome the multiple obstacles. The story of Helen Keller does not seem like another country's example. I am proud of her when I hear about the experiences of my acquaintance who helps multiple disabled people. She and her husband are wonderful teachers like Ann Sullivan. The disabled who have lost both sight and hearing use their hands, touching others' faces in order to recognize and communicate. The story of their daily lives is heartbreaking, and the process of overcoming the multiple disabilities is wonderful and even admirable. They have helped those with multiple disabilities for over twenty years.

As Helen Keller said, when one door of happiness closes, the other door opens and the world can be still filled with power to overcome them even if it is filled with hardships. The disabled people fight daily toward the other side of happiness.

During my visit to Seoul this summer, I set my small donation with monthly automatic transfer that can be passed on to those with disabilities. When I came back across the Pacific Ocean. I pondered the fact that a tiny country, South Korea, is a half the size of one small state in the fifty United States, but South Korea seems to be the best country for the people with disabilities. At least there is convenient public transportation which are very easily accessible to them like their feet.

— Nov. 5, 2015

2.8 Call It "Death with Dignity" Or "Murder"

There is a difference between mercy killing and death with dignity. Mercy killing, euthanasia, is defined as 'the act or treatment of patients who are suffering from painful incurable disease or physical illness, leads to death without any pain', but it ends life by an artificial act before natural death. On the other hand, death with dignity accepts natural death by stopping unnecessary life-saving treatment when the death is imminent even though he or she has medical treatment, that is, by stopping nutrition and medication necessary for maintaining life. This is also called passive euthanasia.

The current law and a legal precedent (case laws) states that "medical staff should do their best to extend their patient's life even for a minute," but active euthanasia is widely accepted by injecting a drug to stop the patient's life, in the United States. Passive euthanasia, removing patient's artificial respiration, is also admitted by 'Advance Directives under the Patient Self-Determination Act' (PSDA). This decision-making system by PSDA, which states that human beings have the right to self-determination to choose the way of their death, and that none of them can be restricted, can result in unreasonable and confusing cases.

This evening, my longtime friend in South Korea sent me a message, 'Friend, my pretty mother went to heaven last night.' The news brought tears to my eyes and I wished to give my friend a big hug and comfort her for her loss. When I worked in South Korea, we could meet any time, share, and comfort each other, exchanging our sorrow and joy.

It was exactly thirteen years ago, April 2003. My friend's mother had just retired from a public school system and visited her daughter for a while. Then, she fell down and into a coma. Three brain surgeries made her mother's forehead seem hollow, badly disfigured(looked ugly). However, she was still unconscious. My friend took her mother from the hospital and looked after her. She hired full-time caregivers, but caring for patients in a coma was too hard. Caregivers did not last long. Fortunately, she was able to hire and keep a good caregiver beside her mother with a higher salary, good work conditions, letting her work strictly from nine in the morning until five in the evening, and off during the weekends. In evenings and on weekends, my friend, after work, always cared for her mother, along with her family.

My friend's care for her mother was impressive indeed. She carried on conversation with the unconscious mother as if she were a conscious and normal person. When I called her "Mom, my friend, Soonie, you know that she is studying in a Ph.D program in the United States, right?" Then, she also asked me to talk to her mother. I said, "How are you, mother? How about your feeling?" I also continued to talk to her as my friend did, even though she was unresponsive to me. After a year, my friend still did not give up, caring for her mother in a coma. Before going to work, she hugged her mother and kissed her cheeks. After work, she told her mother in the evenings what happened at work that day. When she bathed her comma state mother, she treated her like a newborn baby from the bottom of her heart.

Two years later, in 2005, my friend's family and people around her started losing hope for her mother's recovery. One day, she said, "My friend, Soonie, I believe that if I were not her daughter, it would not be possible to nurse her in a coma over a year, without giving up."

In February 2006, a miracle occurred to her mother who spent three years on a bed in a coma. She woke up and could slowly move around. She could read books again and eat regular meals. She was happy, even using the wheelchair because of her weakened legs. In September 2015, when I visited South Korea, her mother was glad to see me. She greeted me in English to make me laugh, not using Korean.

In my friend's mother's case, her family and doctors had stopped the medical treatment of her mother in a coma, called 'death with dignity, passive Euthanasia,' taking away the medical equipments needed to maintain her life thirteen years ago, would it have been a death with dignity or a murder? Also, my niece in an elementary school was in a coma for a year after she was involved in a traffic accident during her family trip. However, her mother wished for recovery and gave her sincere care. After a year, she woke up again and became healthy. My niece is now a mother of two children.

Whenever I think of the mysteries of our human bodies, I recall the words from my high school teacher, the "genius" physicist, who had so much knowledge, "All knowledge we learn or know is only a tiny dust in our gigantic universe." Thus, supporters of death with dignity or mercy killing should reconsider and carefully decide because our human bodies are very mysteries and medical technology can not be reached to the myth, challenging ethics and moral issues. We must always keep in mind that all lives must be valued and not neglected.

— Feb. 24, 2016

2.9 Popular Korean Fast-Food, RaMyun

RaMyun is one of the most popular instant noodle in South Korea.
Tens of RaMyun types are on the shelves in any stores. But I do not
like RaMyun or any type of food made with flour because I had too
many flours based foods in my childhood. When I look at the flour
food, the memories of my hard days come back.

In the dark days of our society in 1970s, the aftermath of the Korean
War, the memories of our long suffering during those days that were
forgotten seem to again overlap with the flour food. Even though I live
in the United States, where flour is major food resources, I try to avoid
eating this kind of flour food if possible.

When I was planning to study in the United States about 20 years
ago, my friend was worried about my eating habits and said to me,
"Hey, how can you survive in the U S where the major food is made
with wheat flour?" In fact, it was one of the hardest parts for me to
live in U.S college dormitory. Instead of bread, I ate American rice,
which had very different taste from Korean rice, with green vegetables
and pepper and cucumber pickles. When I had to eat a hamburger

sandwich in meetings, I had to swallow it with difficulty, along with a cup of drink as if I were taking bitter medicines.

Amazingly I was slowly adapting myself to the very different American culture and food. It proved that human beings are amazed at their adaptability to a very different environment. At first, it was painful like eating bitter medicine, but few years later it was just like eating a tasteless medicine. With time, I am getting accustomed with flour food as I live longer in America.

One of flour foods, Korean RaMyun is one of things I do not like very much. Ironically, when I introduced it to my American husband to check if he was interested in, he did like it because it was spicy, invigorating (refreshing) unique taste, made by flour. At first, every time he took one bite, he had tears, he had to drink several cups of water by the spicy taste, but he seemed to enjoy the taste, calming his burned lips, surprised by the spicy taste.

He loves the RaMyun noodle and I make it for him when he is not feeling good. I am very grateful that I can make him feel better with my little effort. Tonight, he felt exhausted by the tiredness and stress from his work. RaMyun's hot, refreshing unique and spicy taste helped him feel better. In fact, the Koreans' favorite noodle stands for a mixture feeling of poor Koreans' history after Korean War.

Professor Marvin Harris, author of *The Riddle of Food Culture*, says that understanding the others' food culture helps them understand the difference. In other words, the culture of the people has led their food culture. Even in the summer, when you need to take protein, beef is so expensive, so eating chicken was a way of life that comes from their social, economic culture. RaMyun is a reminder of economically difficult period, the aftermath of the war in the 1960s.

— Apr. 1, 2014

Chapter III

Korean Culture to the World

3.1 Everyone Knows Samsung, But South Korea

Americans often eats out once or twice a week. It is not rare to have to wait 30 minutes or longer in a good restaurant, especially on weekends. An Italian restaurant we often go to is famous for its taste, service, prices, and relaxing atmosphere, and we often have to wait for an hour or longer on weekends. It was very hard for me to adapt myself to this culture of waiting because I used to first make reservations before going to any restaurant in South Korea. Whenever we have wait for a long time, I thought that Koreans manage their time more wisely. Restaurant employees usually help us to wait at the restaurant bar in its entrance area. We can first sit down and drink comfortably while waiting for a table.

After church on Sunday, many Americans enjoy dining out with their families. Sunday dining-out seems to be part of American culture and lifestyle. One Sunday, as we were waiting for a table at a restaurant, with many other people in a crowded bar, I saw a young couple doing something fun with a Samsung Galaxy phone. They seem very happy with their phone and I was curious to see how much they knew about South Korea.

"Do you know which country made your new phone?" I asked the girl.
"I do not know." she replied.
"South Korea!" I said
"Is that right?" she responded.

I was surprised and somewhat disappointed by her reaction. She showed me as if my question was nothing important; as if Samsung and South Korea were not related at all. She didn't seem to care that Samsung is a Korean company.

"I'm from South Korea. Your phone is a product of our country." I said.
"Yeah?" she replied.

Americans sometimes do not seem to be interested in which country makes what product because there are so many nationalities living in America and a lot of imported goods and products. Americans seem to be only interested in the quality of a product. It does not seem to matter where it is made in or what region or country it comes. When I first drove a Volvo, I assumed Volvos were produced in the US, so I thought it was an American car. Later, I learned that it had been made in Sweden. Just like this, Americans only seem to care about the product, not its origins in South Korea.

However, the South Korean government supports and backs Korean corporations as a national major project. Thus, Koreans have a national expectation and pride about these large corporations such as Samsung, Hyundai, LG, and so on. Koreans have learned and are accustomed to thinking that growing our corporations is equal to growing the international power of South Korea. Large corporations make big profits and are wealthy, but Koreans believe that large corporations are patriots and give them credit for improving the Korean economy.

Americans, which meet diverse races and many different imported products from all over the world, do not seem to think of direct connection of the business products to their countries of origin as we do. They don't seem conscious of corporations' power as it relates to US wealth.

When I say that I am from South Korea, the first thing Americans often ask me is, "What do you think about North Korea?" I learned that Americans have more interest in North Korea than South Korea. People have sometimes described how crazy and dangerous North Korean leaders Kim Jong Il and Kim Il Sung were, even though I did not even ask. In fact, we have been constantly hearing about the dangers of North Korea over decades. Thus we are now not as sensitive to it as Americans might think. In fact, many South Koreans are insensitive to the danger of North Korea. What is most surprising is that even though the United States is the closest ally of South Korea, Americans do not know nor care about South Korea as much as we think of Americans.

A college girl I met in my Doctoral program said that her grandfather was in the Korean War a long time ago. She heard that toilets there were unique. In the 1970s, toilet, especially, in rural areas, were truly primitive, and this girl knew only of 1950s'-era Korea, learning from her grandfather's experiences, even though she was living in the 2000s. And she treated me as if I was from the 1950s, as well. She was surprised that when I said that what she had said was a fact of the 1950s and not the 21st century.

Modern South Korea has similar economic, social, and cultural systems to the US. Americans are not interested in learning about Korea, so they do not understand Korea's progress and evolution in economical, political, and cultural matters. Thus, I realize that educating foreigners on South Korea is a responsibility of next generation.

After listening to the girl's witness about her grandfather's story and Korea, I went to a bookstore in town and tried to find how many books were there about my country, South Korea. Even in the largest bookstore, Barnes & Noble, I could not find any good reference books on Korea. I was surprised to find only a few outdated ones, for example, simple travelers' guides. The tourist guide booklets were published a long time ago, far from the reality of modern South Korea.

In the bookstore I again realized why our country was unknown to westerners. Before I say that they are simply indifferent, I should have recognized that we did not take any effort to educate and inform the reality of 21st-centurySouthKorea.

Since Samsung is such a big company that the Korean government has supported to grow and develop, it should have also taken the lead in advertising and informing American and the world about the revolution of South Korea. Our government should also try to inform and spread the word about the advanced Korea more aggressively and systematically.

— May 5, 2014

3.2 February, Black History Month

Last month, US State Department deputy head, Antony Blinken, said, "Do not mention the South Korean comfort women issue anymore." He probably could not understand the depth of Korean's wounds scared by their wars. I have been living in America for a long time and I have only recently learned about the history of black people through the document which showed the carved into the bones of ethnic minorities.

Therefore, I would like to take a few notes from the voices of observers who have directly experienced the Japanese 's accomplishments during the Japanese colonial period (1909-1945), to help the mainstream intellectuals and politicians of the United States understand Koreans better.

Decades after the end of the war, in 1970, teachers in my elementary school taught students by using a mixture of fluent Japanese and Korean. Although they use a fluent Japanese language, they were native Koreans born and raised in Korea. Japan invasion For 36 years, Japan forced all Koreans use only Japanese by supervising and educating them to use only Japanese language instead of Korean. The fluent Japanese language skills of my teachers were sadly to me as proof of the atrocities of Japan. I can imagine that Russia can colonize the United States so that only Russian can be used, and that all American politics, society and culture are made into Russia. It would be horrible.

After a few decades, the adults who had lived in the Japanese colonial period declared their pain to the young people in a word, "The Japanese were not like human." For a more detailed account, the Japanese went into Korean homes and took all the items needed for war, such as precious brassware used in all ironware and sacrifices of the ancestors, and used them for World War II. Not only that, but all the food that could sustain life was also robbed, and our people had to fill up their hunger with the fatigue. I can imagine that the Russians used all the tools and food Americans had in the United States for war, and Americans had to eat the roots of trees. Just imagine it makes me sick.

All of Korea 's politics, culture, and social systems were changed into Japanese systems, and healthy Korean men were drafted to China area for war which was very cold. Young women were also dragged into the name of comfort women, and most of the news became unknown. After robbing and exploiting all this, the survivors were always told that even after decades they could not forget the pain of the time. I think the Russian army forced the Americans and took young girls aged 13 to 14 and used them as sexual slaves. It is a trembling thing.

The excuse that the Japanese government recently made about the comfort women sacrificed in the Second World War is trying to cover the sky with the palms of the hands. The fact that there is no evidence that the Japanese military forced to cooperate with the comfort women is derived from the supremacy of Japan's sovereignty in Japan, It is only a result. Japan would have to be forgiven only by acknowledging the mistakes like Germany and reflecting and apologizing to a number of victims including the Second World War victims. Why does Japan "take it right" and do not regret and apologize for the many cruel crimes committed in Asia, especially into the comfort women.

In the United States, February is the Black History Month. Recalling it in February, the wounds of the wartime and the atrocities of the comfort women can be healed by the apology as well as astronomical monetary rewards. Japanese leaders also should accept historical facts. The issue of comfort women should be resolved quickly by apology. It is deeply rooted in the minds of Koreans, and almost sore wounds and hoping that the murmur "The Japanese were not people" will be wiped out .

—Jan. 31, 2016

3.3 Annandale Village

I discovered a unique place called Annandale Village, when my husband and I went there to participate in a training session as Special Olympic leaders. It is located a half-mile from Satellite Boulevard in Suwanee. It is a quiet, clean, and fully-equipped small village in a wooded area, and an exemplary social service facility for adults with developmental disabilities.

The facility offers a variety of programs that allow students with disabilities to graduate from public secondary schools, and become self-reliant adults. The various sports, arts and crafts are therapy and hobby as well. On-site caregivers and medical staff manage the residents' health. It is a heavenly place, with a beautiful residential complex of clean and comfortable houses that are widely-spaced. Adults with developmental disabilities who live with their parents or guardians in the local community can come to the social service facilities here and participate in the programs as well. Some patients are able to obtain full- or part-time jobs through this program. Anyone living in Annandale Village or who is participating in the program is able to actively engage in activities in community clubs, sports groups, or churches. Public institutions such as hospitals, schools, and libraries are also located near Annandale Village. Residents can use them whenever they need, and they can earn regular income by finding jobs that suit their needs. I was very impressed by this nice facility and its programs.

Recently, the number of people with developmental disabilities or with brain damage caused by accident or disease has increased. Annandale Village offers a variety of programs to help such people with severe brain damage dealing with their disabilities. The resources the facility uses are mainly made up of taxes, donations, and a small amount of fees paid by the residents.

Financing of such social service programs is a point of political debate, However, when we think of welfare facilities such as Annandale Village, we should also consider aiming at a society where all members live together well. To that end, I may feel more comfortable in that my taxes be used to help those in need - desperate neighbors, the disabled, or the elderly. If our taxes are used to help people with brain damage or developmental disabilities in social service facilities like Annandale Village, we may be proud of ourselves, because we are contributing to making our society better.

An acquaintance whom I met at church says, "We were not put on this Earth to own our property, we're just here to manage the property." At the time of our leaving this world, another manager takes over and manages the assets we used to manage. This acquaintance has decided to donate his assets (except for the cost of their children's education) to a social service facility as his next "property manager."

Everyone is born empty-handed and dies empty-handed. In other words, when we leave this world, we leave everything behind. We even leave our bodies. But we forget this fact. If we think of this truth through meditation even once a day, the facilities like Annandale Village can increase and prosper, and eventually our world will be closer to a fully-equal society.

—Jun. 5, 2016

3.4 Japanese Language in Elementary Classroom, Remnants of Japan's Invasion Period

"Ichi, ni, san, shi, go, roku…"

The sound of children repeating numbers in Japanese emanated from elementary school classrooms in South Korea in the 1970's. These children had never experienced the Korean situations during World War II, nor a Japanese colony, but were still being taught by teachers who were educated during that period. At that time Japanese was an official language that public school teachers used to count the number of young elementary students in a classroom.

I therefore had the opportunity to learn Japanese in school.

My teacher had been born and raised in the Japanese colonial period, World War II, in Korea. He had to learn Japanese language and culture in Korea under Japan's political rule. He was one of our older generation, parents and grandparents, who inherited the legacy of Japanese language and the Japanese culture. Korea was Japanized during the colonial period. I was from the post-war generation who were still influenced by my teachers, the remnants of Japan's colonization. School children in the post-war period continued to learn such colonial culture from teachers who still spoke Japanese in their daily life even after the end of the colonial period.

In my teens, when I began to learn and understand our history with Japan, I felt disgusted at everything related to Japan because of it. I learned the true history and Japan's cruelty to our ancestors. I heard the anger and regret of Japanese people, describing how cruel they were for 36 years in Korea. My town, Gyeongju, was a hot spot for tourists. Most of the tourists in the 1970's and 1980's were Japanese, but I always thought of the Japanese people as a bad island people.

In high school, I had no choice but to learn Japanese as a second language. Japanese class was not fun to me at all. I was not proud of myself for learning Japanese. I was never interested in visiting Japan even though Tokyo was a nearby airport transit zone, and easy to get to. To me, Japan might have been physically the nearest neighboring country, but it was the farthest country on earth from me.

If the aftermath of the Korean War was economic and physical destruction. Japan's invasion of Korea and its colonial rule destroyed even much more of Korea and its cultural and spiritual life. The remnants of Japan left in Korea can be easily found in many places, including language, culture, politics, education system, and so on. For example, cherry blossoms bloom beautifully in Spring. It is easy for us to forget, because the flowers are so pretty and smell so good, that these were brought by the Japanese. On March 1st, many organizations are busy with events to commemorate Korea becoming free of Japanese rule.

But It has been argued that we should not hate Japan too much and we have to learn its strengths and beat them economically. The idea that we should learn Japan's strengths and that we should surpass Japan gave us a chance to think of productive ways of developing international relationships and to take a neutral stance, separate from our emotional feeling toward Japan.

In fact, the Korean economy is outpacing Japan these days. We survived Japan's invasive political ambitions, rose from the ruins of war, and are on the ranks of world economic power. I think this big change was possible because we maintained the spirit of nonviolence seen in the March 1st Movement of protest against Japan in 1919, and the sacrifices of our ancestors.

— Mar. 3, 2014

3.5 A True Victory

A few weeks ago I visited a Korean church. In his sermon, a pastor in the church spoke about the dissatisfaction in our society these days.

"Do you like the pastor in your church? If you don't like him, you should respect him more. Treat a pastor better and say more good words about him and spread them. Then, at the end, not only within the church, but also in the region, his reputation improves, and he whom you do not like, naturally becomes famous. Then, other churches try to invite him. Then he will be promoted to go somewhere else and you will eventually rejoice. "

I empathize deeply with the pastor's words. We have to be objective and sound critics, but often express personal emotional feelings. So we hurt both ourselves and others, and ultimately have bad results for everyone. If we praise and spread positive words about each other, it will bring good results not only to those who we dislike, but to ourselves as well. Would this be a true victory?

A true victory is that everyone becomes a successful person. If you attack or criticize each other without evidence, rather than productive debate based on facts, your opponent will hurt you and you will be hurt as well. It is easy to overlook that, like the pastor's sermon, respecting and even complimenting your opponent brings good results to yourself.

I wake up around 5:30 every morning. Unless I am hospitalized, I prepare breakfast every morning for my husband while he gets ready for work. On cold days on early mornings, I really don't want to get up. I get the same feeling after we have a big argument, but I always get up and prepare for his breakfast for him. I help him wake up, clearing his head with hot coffee, opening his sleepy eyes. I prepare three or four fresh boiled eggs every morning because he still wants to build his muscles like professional body builders. I give him oatmeal mixed with dried peaches and beans because it is a nutritious food that not only reduces his weight but also lowers cholesterol. I also give him fresh fruits that are high in vitamins.

I do this even when I don't want to talk to him because of an argument. No one would believe that all I do for him is purely for myself; that suppressing my feelings and praying for him to have a good day is really all for myself. When he has a pleasant day, the positive impact comes back to me. If you treat partner well, being patient, he will have time to think, and at the end he will have time to realize his mistakes.

Thinking twice and forgiving can be in fact good for ourselves. People do not easily realize the truth that if I point a finger at others, the remaining three fingers point back towards me.

Regarding social issues, it seems that even our global village is suffering from social dissatisfaction. In the United States, street protests are spreading, with all kinds of complaints, such as the Black Lives Matter movement. Protests are sometimes accompanied by violence and riots to promote social chaos. Similar things happen around the world.

When I turn on the computer or the television, the events that pour out seem to show a nuclear explosion of dissatisfaction. These days I feel that leaving man-made civilization, touching the soil like our ancient ancestors, and living in nature seems to be a happier and more peaceful life. But before I burst out, the pastor reminds me that if I respect the one I don't like, it will return to me with a positive result.

— Nov. 22, 2016

3.6 Name Torture

Born in a small country town in the south of Korea in the 1960s, I grew up in a thoroughly Confucian and patriarchal social setting that respected and prioritized men. The lack of human rights for women, though, was apparent even in the naming conventions of the time. When a boy was born, the adults proudly placed their genealogy on their door, searching for a naming expert and giving the child the best name that would shine the glory of the family for a long time. When a girl got married, however, she had to take her family register with her, so she was considered a permanent member of her husband's family. As a result, my parents copied a name "Soon-Hee", which is very common and easy to call for a girl, without using professional's help.

When I was in elementary school, I was surprised by boys with playing and teasing me with my name, "Soon-hee-ya, let's play" quoting a line from our Language Arts textbook. Passing through the hallway, the boys repeatedly shouted out, repeating the phrase, "Soon-hee-ya, let's play," "Soon-hee-ya, let's play," They enjoyed screaming out my name nearby me. The anger I felt at that time still seems to remain, and I used to blame my parents.

In my adolescence, I went to a Catholic High School, rejected my father's strict rules, and turned to Catholicism. I also got baptized and got a new name, Clara. My father, a minister at church, was very upset, and his feeling carried on for 20 years. Most of the priests and church people liked to call me Clara instead of Soon Hee. I enjoyed being in the church. In the 1980's and 1990's, students in my English class often had one English name, so Clara was used more naturally by students who were learning English in my class.

Recently, a financial institution in the United States asked for a name on my credit history. Korea never uses abbreviations of names in banks or public institutions. In the United States, names are used on social security cards, driver's licenses, and passports. Recently, however, it seems that many financial institutions in the United States do not manage their customers' names correctly.

The problem with names on my credit history starts with cultural differences when I applied for a graduate program in the United States 20 years ago. When I wrote my name on a college application in Korea, "Soon Hee Kwon" in English, Americans in many cases interpreted to Soon Kwon, assuming that Hee was my middle name, and omitting it. So I had to use "Soonhee" Kwon without spaces between Soon and Hee. Then I get married and, following Western culture, added my husband's name to my last name, becoming Clara Soonhee Kwon-Tatum. But some banks record only Clara Tatum and omit all middle names. I asked for a hyphen (-) between Kwon and Tatum, hoping that my Korean identity could appear in my name.

Thus, I always hope to see my Korean identity in my name records as written on my bank documents.

In recent years, personal information management in the US government and in financial institutions seems to have become worse. In terms of personal security, we should pay more attention to name management.

Credit reports sent by banks show a variety of names, regardless of the social security card or driver's license I trusted and submitted; the middle name abbreviated in some banks or omitted all in other banks. Why aren't there many banks that record my full name as Clara Soonhee Kwon-Tatum? This institutional error can be used for crime and the damage will be left to us, very sadly.

— Feb. 16, 2017

3.7 Translating Korean Poetry vs. the Nobel Prize in Literature

"Have you ever eaten persimmons?"

"No."

"This is a Korean persimmon; try it."

I was offering my husband some persimmon; a ripe soft one, a big one, a sweet hard one, and my favorite, a dried one. He said, "It's tasty and great. It's not like the ones in here America."

My husband, a native southern American, was amazed he tasted the Korean persimmons, each of which has a different taste. He admires the taste of the various Korean persimmons. There are many stories about Korean lives and culture related to persimmons; they are a deeply-rooted part of our society. How can Westerners understand Korean culture if they do not know the unique taste of persimmons?

There are still many persimmon trees in South Korea. In Spring, when I was a little girl, my friends and I used to make necklaces from persimmon flowers; in Summer we could avoid the hot sun, sat down on a mat, and played with school friends in the shade under a persimmon tree. We played on the mat or did school homework with friends, listening the sound of Cicadas hiding and chirping on the persimmon leaves. In Fall, we had another pleasure, climbing on persimmon trees and picking the ripe persimmons on the tree covered by Fall frost.

Hongsi, soft ripe persimmons, stored in big jars during cold long winter, was special winter snacks for the elderly, the sick, and for children with their weak teeth. We spent the long winters enjoying eating them as our winter snacks. It was also a part of our unique culture, to see peeled persimmons hanging out on strings to dry in the open air on a sunny side of a house. Dried persimmons were popular to quiet a crying child, and they were also used for rituals and holiday events. Sweet persimmons were a winter snack for everyone in Korea. We never forget the moments that we used to pull off the stem of a Hongsi and enjoyed eating it during the harsh winter weather inside a warm room, heated by Ondol (hot water pipes under the floor).

I recognized that it would be very difficult for Westerners to understand this facet of Korean culture and the emotional attachment of Koreans to persimmons when I began translating Korean contemporary poems to English. For example, Jang Seok-ju's poem, "Dan-gam," which means a sweet persimmon, expresses the dried stem of a sweet persimmon as its navel, "Where once ten thousand springtimes passed and where the universe gushed in." When I read this poem, I reflect on Korean culture and the large number of stories related to the Korean persimmons.

However, it is impossible for Westerners to feel the poem the same way Koreans do and to enjoy persimmons as we do, because they do not eat persimmons as much as we do. Experts might research and study our culture through books and educational materials in order to understand Korean poetry. Ordinary foreign readers who are pursuing their busy daily lives might find it very difficult to study Korean culture and find materials sufficient to understand Korean poetry.

Translation of Korean poetry must convey into other languages a condensed form of Korean culture in a few words. Poetry translators have to study Western or European culture and literature and translate our poems to English from their standpoints, with or without a full understanding of Korean culture. However, there is a "cultural gap" in many readers' understanding of cultural differences. Therefore, it would be almost a miracle if Westerners came to admire Korean poets and award them their Nobel Prizes.

It is very difficult to translate the culture and emotions expressed in Korean poetry into English with short phrases so that foreigners can enjoy Korean poems themselves. Just as Americans here in Georgia do not eat persimmons, our culture of such foods cannot be understood clearly by non-Koreans. This reminds me of someone's honest remarks that it would be very difficult for a Korean poet to receive a Nobel Prize.

Poetry is a culture. Our poetry is a matter of releasing our culture and emotions. So it is enough for us to hold and enjoy our own literacy festivals.

— Oct. 6, 2016

3.8 Korean Literature Translation and Sharing Korean Culture

There is a common question that Americans used to ask me whenever I say that I am from South Korea. It is about how we live in constant fear of possible invasion by North Korea. The main concern from the Americans I learned is the North Korean threat to South Korea. They seem to know North Korea better than Koreans do and care for our country more than we Koreans do.

This is not surprising, due to the power of the mass media in the United States, where 99 of 100 news stories about Korea relate to North Korea's possible threat to South Korea. In addition, Americans generally do not know much about South Korea nor are they interested in much of the political issues around the world. Many Americans even do not know the exact names of important leaders in the USA; they seem mainly interested in sports and shopping.

Americans use Samsung's televisions and its cell phones every day, but they are indifferent as to the origin of these products, South Korea. They may not even know where Korea is located on the world map. If Koreans knew this, they would be surprised, but it is a reality.

Americans seem to acknowledge South Korea as a military ally that is currently threatened by North Korea and Koreans are absolutely in need of US help, which is why the US sends troops to maintain peace in Korea.

When I went to a bookstore to find educational materials about Korea for Americans, only a few books were available, most of which were written a long time ago. Even in the database of the largest public library in southern Georgia, literary works or translated books written by Korean authors are very few and all I could find were few books such as ones written by Krys Lee, Chang-Rae Lee, and Soonja Kwon. Fewer than ten titles are available.

When I came to study here in the USA 20 years ago, I thought I would be able to achieve anything with pride and I was proud of being a Korean then. The longer I stay, I find myself feeling less and less proud of the political status of Korea to the rest of the world. China is, culturally, 20 to 30 years behind Korea, but China's political status in the United States and world seems to be 20 to 30 years ahead of that of Korea. In the fall of 2015, a Boston writer asked me to take part in a project called "Korean Literature to the World" when I was studying and concerned about Korea's political status. Our team actively participated in promoting real Korean life and spiritual culture. I needed a native speaker's help in translating Korean literature to English so I looked for writers who might be interested in Korean literature in the American Literature Group in which I have participated for many years. I couldn't find a single person I could work with.

The translation of Korean poetry could help explain the Korean view of life, as deeply related to the Korean people's spiritual culture, which is never really shown in the media, being overshadowed by the threats of North Korea. I believe that foreigners could feel and understand our unique culture and life better through an understanding of Korean literature. In order to introduce Korean literature to the world, translators need to be proficient in both English and Korean, and to have the ability to understand and digest both English and Korean literature as it reflects Korean culture, not simply translating word-for-word and hoping that readers will understand better. In-depth knowledge of the culture is necessary to aid in proper translation of poetry.

This year marks a half-century of Korean immigration to Atlanta. I know that individuals, organizations and government agencies in Atlanta have worked tirelessly to raise Korean pride with a variety of activities. In this 50th year of Koreans coming to Georgia, Macro Education Institute is receiving applications for its first competition for translation of Korean poetry and literature. This event will provide us with the opportunity to share Korean culture with people from other countries as well as those who are ignorant of Korea. We also believe that outreach through events such as this competition will give non-Koreans a chance to understand and communicate with Koreans and their community better. Our team hopes that this event will find excellent second- and third-generation translators who can contribute to promoting our culture and enhancing and explaining our values and pride.

— Feb. 3, 2017

3.9 Official vs. Unofficial (1)

I used to be actively involved in a local literary organization, which, like many such organizations, was a small, unofficial nonprofit group that collected monthly membership fees for activities, for donating to good causes, and for publishing members' works. Prior to being registered as an official nonprofit in the state of Georgia in 2016, it was what accountants call a "ghost organization," because it did not report any of its finances to the IRS. I dislike this attitude toward small nonprofit organizations, so I spent the last few weeks consulting and doing research regarding nonprofit organizations in the US.

There are of course a great many unofficial nonprofit organizations, such as alumni organizations, poetry societies, sports gatherings, walking clubs and so on. They meet regularly, pool money for activities, help the needy and host special events for their local communities. In American society, where helping people is the norm, there are countless such unofficial nonprofit organizations. The lives of American people are filled with small organizations that fundraise for the needy, quilting groups, choirs, reading clubs, orchestras, weekly golf gatherings, bike clubs, motorcycle meet-ups, antique car fanatics and more. However, these, too, are considered ghost organizations by tax accountants because they do not report operations or finances.

How can the American government legitimize all these organizations? According to my research, small nonprofit organizations that make an annual profit of less than $5,000 qualify under 501(c)* regulations to receive tax benefits, both for the organization and the people involved – a byproduct of the American government's recognition of citizens intending to help others.

While researching into nonprofits, I was reminded of a story my childhood science teacher told me. A serious scientist once brought his microscope, meant for bacterial research, into his home and saw how every appliance and all his food was teeming with bacteria. He developed a morbid fear of these germs, stopped eating, and starved to death.

The lesson is that bacteria coexists with us and will continue to do so; it's inescapable, and actually often beneficial — you shouldn't try to avoid it. Similarly, these small nonprofit organizations, even if they are incorporated and don't pay taxes, do a lot of good, and should be left alone to operate — we shouldn't refer to them as "ghost organizations."

3.10 Official vs. Unofficial (2)

I tear up whenever I hear of disabled and abandoned Korean children being adopted by faraway American families during the 1980s, when the Korean economy wasn't developed enough to support these children, even after Korean War in 1950s. The American families showed true humanity by providing not only economic and educational support, but also medical support to give a second chance at life to these adoptees, through surgery and healthcare.

Americans' Christian love carries over to animals as well. Every region has a shelter to take care of and treat for sick animals. It is common to see neighbors taking sick animals on walks in a stroller. Some carry pretty little bags on these walks and inside are cleaning supplies to clean up after their dogs. It's much like a parent who carries all the things needed to take a child outside. This philanthropy towards even animals shows American society's attitude towards unofficial charity work.

However, an acquaintance who has worked in other community for a long time told me that some charities are created simply in order to receive financial aid from the government.

As a matter of fact, a lot of changes have taken place among charities within the last few years. Some initiatives that are spread throughout big cities like New York include federal aid for housing, pre-school, after school programs, Title I, nursing programs, career guidance for single mothers and more.

On the other hand, federal aid for retired and disabled veterans has been greatly reduced. Instead, advertising the charities helping these veterans has mysteriously increased. For senior welfare, it has gotten to the point where some people joke that an elderly person would be better off in prison, given the federal cuts in medical care.

A parenting program in the Macro Education Institute that I've directed for several years is called "Bedtime Reading." It was created in an effort to reduce teenage violence resulting from domestic problems through social educational approaches and to encourage deep conversations between a parent and child, thus improving both their relationship and society at large. Through this program, I found out more about a gigantic charity organizations the Salvation Army. Every region's branch of the Salvation Army receives donations from their own communities without getting any help from the Salvation Army headquarters, which we often see advertised on TV or other media outlets. I, too, did not get any help for my program from the Salvation Army organization and received help and donations from my own local libraries and churches while covering the rest of the expenses from my own pocket.

No one knows where the aid and donations the central Salvation Army receives from its worldwide marketing are being used. It probably has nothing to do with the local Salvation Armies that we know of. Recently, a person in the medical field informed me that a lot of times, heaps of precious medical supplies donated to Undeveloped countries immediately get robbed by terrorist organizations or gangs as soon as it arrives in the countries, and the local residents don't receive the actual help that they desperately need. In order to prevent misusing donations in the charities, we must track — or at least be cautious of — where every cent of our donations ends up.

Chapter IV

Sharing Different Culture

4.1 Selective Perception : Joy of Able to Forget

Many people envy those with particularly retentive memories. But as we get older, we realize that forgetting is another positive aspect of humans. Forgetting protects us from stress and is vital to our survival. Hee-taek Lim, the author of The Joy of Forgetting, says that forgetting is like clothes that protect us from external impact. It is said that memory hinders happiness, and those who forget well can be freshly happy every day.

When I last visited my country, I met an old friend for the first time in a long time. As comfortable as we've always been, we enjoyed chatting, reminiscing about our childhood. During the conversation she talked about how she still resented the very mischievous behavior of one of her school classmates. The fact that she was still not forgetting surprised me. I had to accept our differences again, realizing that we were looking at the same problem from very different perspectives and ideas. This boy harassed girls with all sorts of very mischievous behaviors, such as spitting food over the girls' clothes or running off after pulling up a girl's skirt. The boy's behavior was weird, mean, and harassing beyond mere mischievousness, such as cutting the girls' jump rope in the middle of their jumping and playing.

However, as I got older, I completely forgot the boy's actions as one-time mischievous behaviors happening in my childhood. I felt that he was just a little child, not knowing much, and not really realizing the bad effects his actions could have had. I therefore forgot the boy's erratic behaviors, but my friend carried it carved on her heart for a long time.

A psychological term used by Professor Oh Jong-suk from Seoul National University, "selective perception," worked on my friend's memory. That is, she has been holding on to these past bad experiences for over 30 years. On the other hand, I forgot all the experiences about the boy's mischievous behaviors as a sort of "selective memory loss." I thought of the boy's actions as simple and meaningless; a little child's mischievous behavior.

As an adult, I face a huge amount of new information every day. We are fortunate to be able to keep our brains healthy in the midst of such a flood of information because we have the function of forgetting. We accept and remember only what is needed as selective perception, out of a great amount of information. Selective perception refers to the selective reception and retention of information based on one's beliefs or values. This act is quite subjective.

In the modern industrial era, advertisements are created in astronomical numbers. It is said that we are exposed to about 1,500 ads a day, of which we perceive only about 76 ads and remember only about 12. Our selective perception functions only accept a few and store them in our brains.

Selective perception and *selective amnesia* are just like two sides of a coin, said a psychologist. Selective cognition and selective memory loss help us stay in a new life, just as we forget the pain of giving birth and thus allow ourselves to be able to give another birth again soon. How many things happen in our lives? Painful events such as unemployment, illness, divorce, death of parents and family, and accidents occur countlessly more often than good things. But with selective cognition we can forget the painful things and live a new life every day.

When I was young, I argued with my brother and sisters, but when I become an adult, I often approach first, apologize, and try to forget, even when my feelings were hurt by conflicts with friends and colleagues. It is my own choice that I try to be free from bad information. I tried to pick up the positives, and accept and store them. I tried to quickly forget; to remove bad information from my memory. Now, when I look at the diary I wrote at that time, I realize that it was nothing. In other words, when looking into the diary, a tool that recalls the past, I often feel that events which were serious in childhood become fun memories over time. Without a diary, my selective amnesia will never remind me of such serious things again.

Choosing, recognizing, and remembering the positive side seems to be vital to my life and to play an important role in making my life healthy. It is essential that you love and care for yourself. People are like reeds, weak and shaken easily and may have conflicts and quarrels with each other, but if we laugh and turn around, shaking hands with each other, we can resolve these conflicts easily. That is, selective cognition that takes the positive side will quickly erase the negative side. This can make our lives easier, especially in the United States with its religious and racial conflicts.

— Dec. 1st, 2015

4.2 An Experimental Trip in an Electric Car

The vehicle market is demanding more eco-friendly electric vehicles that use less oil and make less noise because of consumers' concerns over the high oil price and the depletion of fossil fuels. Depending on the type of vehicle, small electric vehicles can go up to 100 miles on a single charge, but may only be able to go 50 or 80 miles depending on weather, road conditions, and driver's driving habits. This is why it takes a lot of preparation, planning, and patience to prevent problems while driving an electric vehicle. Not many drivers can properly and effectively handle an electric car. In some instances, having an electric car can be impractical and very high-maintenance. This article highlights the issues of driving an electric vehicle.

My husband, who loves his electric car, took me on a tour around Chattanooga during the holiday season. It is about 150 miles from my house. We left home around 12:30 pm to drive to Kennesaw, GA, 50 miles away, but the car alerted us that there was only enough energy for 40 miles. We needed to charge our car before our next destination. Luckily my husband's driving habits are very conservative and we made it to the Kennesaw N Dealer. We planned to use a fast charging station for electric cars. However, there was another electric car using the fast charger in front of us, so we had to wait at least 30 minutes to charge our car. Then, another 40 minutes passed when we were charging our car to have enough energy, up to 80 miles. It took at least an hour to charge our car. First we used the fast charging charger. A typical slower charger would have taken another hour to charge up for only 20 more miles. Without using the fast charger, we could have been stuck at the Kennesaw N Dealer for an extra hour just to charge our car enough for 80 miles of travel.

It was 5 pm when we finished charging his electric car and we finally headed off to our next destination, Dalton. Due to the cold winter weather, the sky was already dark and we needed to turn our headlights on. Additionally, the heater and the window wipers was turned on because it was foggy and raining. Even though we had just charged our car, the car panel alerted us again that there was energy for less than 20 miles. My husband, an expert on electric cars, exited the highway and drove on local roads to save the electric energy because local roads use about 40 to 50 miles of energy per hour while the highway uses 60 to 65 miles of energy per hour. Less than 50 miles away, we found another electric car charging station. We discovered the N charging station in Dalton City, but there was not a quick fast charger and we did not want to wait an additional hour in the dark, cold night. Fortunately there was a personally-operated quick-charger ten miles away. So, we drove ten more miles in the cold, foggy weather and heavy rains, to a standalone quick charger station. The charger was available for $6.99 per a mile energy — a very expensive price compared to gas, but the charger was our savior. It took 40 minutes to charge up enough for 80 miles, and then we went to a nearby hotel at 7:00PM.

The next day at 11am, we spent an hour at a shopping mall near our final destination, then went back to the charging station about 1 pm and then drove to the nearest N dealer, which was very different from the station we thought it would be based on our Internet google search. We had a problem finding the right charging station.

On the way to another N dealer, a sign saying, "Under construction, go back" blocked the way to get the charging station. My husband turned around and barely arrived, but every single quick charger was broken and couldn't be used. He only had 20 miles of energy left and was very nervous with the fear that the car would stop in the middle of the road. The staff said we can find a quick charger on the nearby hotel, so we used GPS to search for the place for more than 30 minutes and then, with barely enough power left, found two regular slow chargers in the hotel parking lot. It took about two hours to charge 50 miles. We were worried about getting back home, so when we arrived in Dalton on the way home, we charged up at the quick charger for 80 miles in about 30 minutes and charged it up to 105 miles over an hour with extra slow regular charging. Before the Kennesaw N dealer closed their door, we arrived. Again, we had to use a quick charger to charge 80 miles in 40 minutes, a regular slow charger over 50 minutes, filled up to 100 miles, and arrived home around10 pm at speeds of less than 60 miles per hour.

What we learned from this trip is that there are many difficulties with having an electric car because the environment we were in has not yet adapted to fulfill the needs of eco-friendly vehicles. However, electric cars will gain popularity when companies and governments install more chargers with lower prices and at comfortable and safe places. Quick car chargers should be placed at least every 20 miles and the cost could be cut in half. Drivers need to carefully plan and prepare for emergencies to prevent the issues, but, my enthusiast husband still praises electric cars. He boasts, "If you charge your car in the garage while you sleep, you do not have to go to the regular gas station in the morning." He says there is no inconvenience in commuting daily by his electric car because his job is within 30 to 40 miles from home.

— *Dec. 28, 2015*

4.3 Valentine's Day Happenings

On Valentine's Day, lovers plan romantic dinners and give each other chocolates or flowers. In the US, people spend $ 18.9 million on Valentine's Day alone. It's a huge shopping day.

J is one of those who have joined this shopping trend. Today is a special day for him: J is an attractive young man in his early 30s with a bright future. He is confident in everything and plans very carefully whenever working. That's why he is also trusted at work. With his professional insight and reasonable mindset, he is popular at work. However, due to his demanding marriage conditions, it is hard to find a good partner.

Today, Valentine's Day, he is more pleased of other days to go to work. He thinks about today's schedule on his way to work. He images that a lot of good things will happen, as on previous Valentine's Days. First, he remembers about a gift from his colleagues last year. He is pleased to think of his manager who cares for him. She always has been extra nice to him and done him a lot of favors. After work, he has an evening appointment with a young woman who met at a church and is looking forward to making future plans. It's still early, but he is planning to propose to her at a special Valentine's Day dinner at his favorite Japanese restaurant. As usual, he enters the company with confidence and sits in his place.

He is called by the manager as soon as he arrives at work. He goes to her office, imagining that she would give him a nice Valentine's Day gift. "The boss and company decided to ask you to resign," she says. The reason is that many people in the company have complained that it is too hard for them to work with J. He was shocked because he never imagined this. The impact might have been greater than it should be because of Valentine's Day. The boss is on a business trip, and J has something of a melt-down until he leaves his office for home. He can't clean the desk right away, so after everyone leaves, he go back to the workplace and cleans up his desk, taking his personal belongings.

He cancels his evening appointment and goes straight home and lies on his bed. He thinks about his workplace, and remembers that he thought he was perfect, but he ignored most of his coworkers, only speaking with some. Although he was fired, he seemed to get a big, unforgettable gift that Valentine's Day: a lesson to be humble, considerate of others, and get along well with his colleagues.

In fact, on Valentine Day, it may be meaningful to think specifically about people who do not have close friends or are not in a good relationship. Surprisingly, as many as 46 percent of Americans say they are not happy with Valentine's Day. There are 153 million orphans around the world who are lonely and have wounded hearts. How about writing a Valentine's love letter to the children who are left alone in an orphanage and hurt? How about reaching out on Valentine's love to a lonely and helpless seniors, an orphan who lost his parents, and people in darkness who are struggling to survive in pain at this moment? Then our society will become much greater place to live.

— Feb. 14, 2016

4.4 A Coffee Cup, Only 70 Percent of Coffee Filled

I start the day serving my husband with his morning coffee. He drinks at least one or two large cups every day. I just fill 70 percent of the cup and take it from the kitchen to the room, so I can walk quickly, avoiding spills. The server and the recipient are both more pleasant. It looks easy, but it is difficult to learn the "70 percent virtue."

John Gray's book, *Men are from Mars, Women are from Venus*, mentions the idea of a "Man Cave." My husband uses the term as if it were his own. Ever since we got married and moved a new home, he has especially emphasized this point. Usually people need a special room because they need their own office, but my husband emphasizes his space, especially using the term "man cave." While using it as a "study and relaxation" space, he decorates his special space with his favorite musical instruments, sports equipment, various books and media, and maintains them to make his own space very comfortable.

He is obsessive on keeping his man's cave a priority, and I didn't understand it at first. I was very curious about his attitude because I thought first that he wanted to hide something from me. But after a long time I watched, it turned out that there was nothing secret stuff. He just wanted to take a nap for day time in his own space and sometimes act like a child. It's hard to keep the pride of a man in front of a woman, so he wanted to do something like this in his own space. After discovering a theory about male psychology which says that men like to share only 70 percent of their thoughts and feelings and hide the other 30 percent, I feel sympathy for the hidden side of maleness.

Before marriage, a man looks like a knight in shining armor, but after marriage, when a couple share their time every day, his bad, weak sides may be discovered. Sometimes he looks like a weak figure that may have his own stress. The same is true of women. They are treated like a princess before they get married, and they are not always treated well after they get married. At this time, we need time and space to think about each other. If a man enters his Man Cave and has the time and space to think alone, this will lead to a healthier couple life. Failure to meet the basic conditions of this human psychology can eventually makes a couple unhappy with each other, and separation or divorce may follow.

When you fill a cup of coffee and stop at 70 percent full, you don't have to worry about spilling it. That 70 percent-full is good to serve every morning. Thirty percent is left as an extra to respect each other. Then there will be no overflowing or damage in marital relationships. In other words, couples should respect each other's time and space.

I remember someone who has had a happy married life for a long time, who said, "For a balanced life between couples, share only 70 percent and keep 30 percent secretly hidden in your own world." It means that we should share 70% of the time, and for the rest, we may take a trip or go shopping, in order to have some time and space for ourselves alone.

You might not want to have 30 percent of your own space to hide or cheat big secrets. You might just want to feel free. This effort makes it possible for couples and friends to be able to create new and stronger relationships, and to maintain long-lasting relationships. This is a virtue of shortage, for a perfect relationship.

— Dec. 26, 2016

4.5 Love for Animals

If you work all day long, you might become exhausted when you come home, but my husband exercises for an hour or two after work every day. Today he also finished his work, took a shower after his workout, and sat at the table for the simple dinner I made. Dinnertime is a precious time to satisfy his hunger. I was away from the dinner table and while I was taking care of something in my office for a while, my husband shouted, "Where did my dinner go?" I looked around the table and found only some pieces of bread scattered on the floor. I could not see any of the meat.

"Oh, no, the dogs ate my meat," he said; but it was unbelievable because our dogs had never done it before. Looking closely again at the crumbs and slices of vegetables scattered on the floor, it was clear, though, that our dogs did. The two tiny Chihuahuas climbed up the chair and ate all the steak. This was the first time the dogs ever touched our food on the table. My hungry husband finished dinner by having only the remaining watermelon and water. He said that he would diet that night. His love for the dogs showed me that he is rarely angered even by their misbehaviors. I felt it long ago when I first met him.

During my studies in the United States, I met my husband and was invited to his parents' house. My husband's parents loved animals, raising two cats and two dogs. Twenty years ago in 1970s, if you were raising a dog in Korea, the dog stayed outside your home. So I was not familiar with American pet dogs being inside, and it was very uncomfortable for me to get close to the cats and dogs my husband's parents keep. Only after his parents had sent all four animals out to the back yard, could I enter the house.

Since then, l have not allowed animals in my home for a long time. I was concerned about the smell and hair from the animals, and having to always prepare food for them, exercise for their health, visit the vet clinic regularly, get regular medical checkups, and medical treatments such as vaccinations. I was not interested in that much work at all.

But love is contagious and since my husband loves dogs, I am slowly changing toward loving dogs. I adopted a dog 6 years ago. Most animal care has been all my job. Because of bathing dogs and cleaning up dog hair every day, I had to clean house more often. Exercising once or twice a day, and preparing snacks made me love the animals more. Our dog looked lonely, so we adopted one more dog. It helps the dogs be healthier and happier because of having another animal around as a friend. My work doubled the burden I have to bear but it's nice to see that the very bad habits that appeared when a dog was lonely, such as biting things and making messes, disappeared.

Another reason Americans like dogs is that they protect owners for security. Raising a dog is better than spending money every month to set up a security system. A dog smells suspicious things outside, pricks up its ears and is alert. When a suspicious person comes near the fence of the house, the dog starts barking. I remember an American friend telling me that if a dog sends a danger signal, then the landlord could prepare a gun for the emergency. She said that a dog and a gun were the best security team.

This evening, my husband is very hungry because of working all day long and doing intense workouts at the gym for an hour or two. He just enjoys playing with the dogs, not even scolding them for stealing his meal. It also seems that my husband's love for animals is completely transferred to me.

— Sep. 2, 2016

Dog lover

4.6 Vietnamese Rice Noodles

Eight years ago, when I first tasted Vietnamese rice noodles, the smell was so disgusting that I left the restaurant after only 10 minutes. I even got upset at a friend who had treated me to the lunch and gave her ugly comments about what she had asked me to eat. It was the first time I ever experienced the aroma of rice noodles, and it was a peculiar and unbearable smell. People who were enjoying the rice noodles in the restaurant seemed to be from a very different world, just like the unfamiliar food. Heedless of my friend's embarrassment, I left the restaurant because I almost had stomach. Later I found out that more and more Koreans are growing to like Vietnamese rice noodles and the number of restaurants are increasing in proportion to its popularity. I could not understand such a change.

Eight years later, I had to go to A Vietnamese rice noodle restaurant again for a business meeting. The acquaintance strongly recommended that I could try the rice noodles, and I forced myself to eat. Then, I looked closely at what was in the meal. It was a very simple dish made with rice flour, noodles, shrimp, raw vegetables, onions, spices, and other condiments. Since then, I tasted it a few more times by my friends' recommendations, and I got used to the aroma, and became familiar with it.

These days, I feel addicted to the special aroma and miss it. So now I go to the rice noodle restaurant on purpose once or twice a month. Surprisingly, when I am hungry, rice noodles come to mind and I start missing the taste and aroma. Fascinated by its unique taste, my mouth and soul are gradually getting used to it. I like it so much that I might be addicted to it.

Bill Phillips, the author of *The Last Diet of My Life*, reports that not only drugs and alcohol are addictive, but also food. It stimulates our brain's addiction centers just as heroin does. There is a way to check if you are addicted: if you can change from the habits by yourself, you are not addicted. If you cannot change yourself from the habit, you are addicted. This month, I think that I should refrain from tasting these noodles, just to see if I am addicted.

We get used to something without knowing it, and we enjoy it slowly. The inadvertent disease of addiction extends not only to alcohol and drugs, but also to our customs, culture, and thinking, including food. Even if it is not really harmful or beneficial to us, it can remind us that our addictions control our minds, and we can become slaves to an object.

—Jan. 9, 2014

4.7 A Glass Ceiling

I watched a TV program on the conventions of both parties, Republicans and Democrats. This time, the Democratic Party is making a historical event on breaking the "Glass Ceiling." On Wednesday night, July 27, the third day of the Democratic National Convention, American women's hearts were beating very fast as Hillary Clinton appeared on the platform and President Obama gave his support to her 2016 presidential election campaign. It was an amazing scene for me to watch Clinton on the most powerful political stage in the world. I had learned that the United States was a more conservative, male-dominated society in political field than Korean society.

Sixteen years ago, I took a deeper look at the inside of the US Congress through a doctoral program on "Women's Politics and Leadership." The United States, which I thought was a country of freedom and equality, passed women's voting rights to the Congress on August 26, 1920, and on August 6, 1965, equal rights were given to all US citizens, regardless of race and gender, and President Lyndon Johnson signed into law that the right to vote is a fundamental right.

When I was young, growing up in a Confucian tradition, I often thought about women's rights. When a boy was born, the family was so happy, and when a girl was born, the opposite was true. A boy tried to educate himself and succeed, by getting the full support from family, friends, and community, even by selling the property of the house, but most of girls in 1970s had to go out to work for the education and success of their brothers. Some of my relatives said, "I do not understand why women educate themselves since they married and become other family members by Confucian tradition" My father was a pastor, so I could go to college, along with two of my sisters. My father persuaded my relatives to say, "Property comes and goes, but learning stays until death, so learning is the best asset."

As I was educated and grew up, I became more interested in extending my education after seeing my grandmothers who were not treated equally. Female friends and seniors who have excelled in all respects have seen their talents postponed after their marriage by childcare and household chores. A young man may praises his wife as "a very smart girl," but after years, the grown girl may give up her career and be struggling with raising her children and house work. Social climate, and entrenched institutions and policies should create a need for us to enable talented women to be able to use their skills.

In Korea, my father's generation was told that when a man works in the kitchen, it was not good and not accepted but my father-in-law, a retired executive of a large American corporation, wears an apron and cooks delicious food for his family. His invitation to me and his children and grandchildren to the supper that he made all for us was a wonderful thing that I saw for the first time in my life. Nevertheless, American society also has a strong glass ceiling in social and political fields. In particular, the social system supporting pregnancy and marriage of poor women is still inadequate.

So, especially last night, I was thrilled to see the Clinton presidential nomination scene. While the Republican nominee, Trump, says he would work for women, but his past life was for himself, Clinton has tried to find human rights and social rights for people with disabilities, for minorities, and for women throughout her life. She has not taken a comfortable, profitable career but has been caring and advocating for outsiders who are struggling without seeing the light in a mainstream society. She has not only talked, but practiced in the field. I think she has the attitude of a true leader regardless of political party and will sacrifice herself for others.

—*Jul. 28, 2016*

4.8 Why We Should Not Live Alone

A few years ago, I noticed an odd gas odor in my house. "Honey, I smell something strange, like chemical smell. How about you?" I asked my husband, as I opened the windows in my house. "Close the window. I'm fine, I do not smell anything," he said. I closed the window and went outside. My husband said, "You are sensitive because you are weak. So you need to go to see your doctor and check your health."

I've been sensitive to taste and smell since I was very young, so if I don't feel fresh air or if I notice an unpleasant smell, I recognize it right away. I have senses as sharp as a dog's. My husband, however, the quality of air and smells. However, Spring and Summer cause him suffering due to allergies, and he is extremely sensitive to pollen. Without taking allergy medication, he is continuously coughing.

Therefore, keeping the windows open would never occur to him and keeping the air conditioning turned on inside house makes him feel happy and pleasant. Many may wonder how two very different people live together. We are so different from basic life style to biorhythms. I called the fire department the next day to find out the reason for the bad smell. Two fire fighters came in and searched inside and outside the house and said they could not smell anything bad. I just had to put on a mask and take care of myself. A few days later my Church friend in my neighborhood came to my house to spend time with me. She did not enter my house, but stood at the door way and said that the smell in my house was so severe that she could not enter. And only after opening all the windows and doors, she could come inside house. I was so glad to have someone as sensitive as me, so I spent time with her, leaving all the doors wide open. I asked her to write a note so that I could show my husband: "The smell in your house is too bad. You should take any action about this issue." I planned to show it to my stubborn husband who does not accept others' opinions. After seeing my friend's note about the smell, my husband finally looked at the air-conditioner filter, and replaced the filter with a new one. I still noticed a bad smell but he seemed not to believe it. I had to sleep with the windows open because it smelled like gas, but my husband closed the window tightly, turned on the air conditioner and slept like baby.

I could not stand the bad air, like odd gas or chemical smell, in my house and I bought the most expensive air purifier. It absorbs all the fine dust and other harmful elements to clear the air. It even sends a danger signal if it senses something dangerous to the human body. Fortunately, the air purifier ran quickly and loudly, sending a red signal as a danger condition of air as soon as I place it into our house. I showed it to my husband, and he looked at it, amazed. With my detailed explanation about the air purifier, he seemed to realize the problem of bad air in the house, but he still couldn't smell anything bad.

The bad smell, gas smell or chemical smell, was felt by people with a keen sense like me, but not dull like my husband's. The average person would feel a little sick, but they might not know why their head hurts. I read an article in an academic journal that minor gas leaks could harden the human's brain a little bit and play a role in causing dementia. I told my husband about the article, and said that he should thank me for preventing him from getting dementia and potentially losing his life. Even when gas leaks, there are people who can't smell it and can die while asleep. These types of incidents are often reported as heart attacks when the weak or elderly pass away while sleeping.

Living alone may be comfortable, but the words from old adults are true: that to live with someone is to help each other when it is dangerous or difficult. Even though we may sometimes regret it when we get married, human beings seem to have to live together.

— Sep. 20, 2016

4.9 Has Violence in Our Society Really Declined?

Steven Pinker, in *The Better Angels of Our Nature*, asks, "Why has violence declined?" — an unusual and controversial question. Pinker says violence is not a "responsive response of our inner characteristics based on our nature," but a "strategic response from the environment in our society," so government intervention plays a large role in reducing human violence.

The birth of a government, the influence of civilization, industrialization, and humanism helped cause a significant decline of violence and crime in our society. Pinker says the temptation to use violence was stigmatized and criminalized. Therefore, violence and crime have been steadily declined along with the "rights revolutions": citizenship, women's rights, children's rights, rights of sexual minorities, and animal rights.

In the 1960s, when I was a child, there were servants in many Korean homes, and a social hierarchy like the caste system in India was present. In the 1970s, however, as our society became industrialized, the servant class became free from their masters and moved into industrial work in the cities.

In the 1980s, by government intervention, South Korea gradually turned into a equal, peaceful society, gradually developing awareness of the rights of women, children, the elderly and the disabled, and wresting those rights from the older male-dominated society. Reflecting on the changes in Korean society, I agree with Pinker's argument.

However, as a country or an organization grows larger, the invisible cancerous powerful groups or organization grows up too, but it is impossible for the government to inspect them all. Thus, much more violence and crime, which are not shown in Pinker's statistics, have occurred and are still happening. Thus, there is a need to show members of a society how to overcome the tragic aggression that causes violence through education at home and in society. Pinker comments that we can avoid or overcome violence and crime with kinship, friendship, empathy through similarity, self-control to prevent harm, and authoritarian Puritan morality.

In the end, however, it is important that we rely on human reason and development of the human reason. I believe that family and society have key responsibilities for building up our rational abilities. Regarding the role of family and society, Kim Hyung-Seok, a 98-year-old writer and scholar, emphasizes ethics, a practical philosophy. Morality, conscience, and ethics should be established more than law based on humanities as an advanced citizen.

Pinker also said that violence and crime have further declined because of technological and electronic revolutions that have enhanced human mobility and thought. In our rapidly evolving and highly information-centric society, all of our lives are occupied by these technologies and tools, and modern people feel the greatest convenience and freedom. However, contrary to Pinker's claim, there are not only small crimes such as e-mail hacking using electronic, but also high-tech crimes that weaken or break high complete security. Hackers steal or manipulate information in military and health care facilities, banks, and government administration data in order to shake up large organizations or other nations. The victims are so widespread that government or organizational investigators are not able to number them. Most of those crimes are not captured by Pinker's statistics.

The crimes enabled by the electronic revolution in our society are far from the limits of government and organization regulations and law. Computer experts say that even Basic instruction in Computer use(Computer 101) can enable a person to penetrate or attack other computers due to the limitations of operating systems. The loopholes and limitations of the Windows OS, for example, almost seem to be a good reason not to use a computer all the time. Pinker also mentioned that these techniques can be catastrophic in modern society. It is to be hoped that a disaster like nuclear terrorism is unlikely to occur.

—Jan. 6, 2017

Chapter V

Living as a Minority

5.1 A Girl in School Cafeteria

In the spring of 1997, when I was still adjusting to my new life as a graduate student in America, I went the school cafeteria for lunch. After putting a few simple things to eat on my tray, I waited behind a long line of students for my turn to pay. I attempted to pay when it was finally my turn, but I was baffled to find out that they only accepted cash. When I looked around, all I saw were tall students who had large eyes, noses, and bodies; even their cups were two, three times larger than mine was, and made me self-conscious. In this uncomfortable situation, I felt that everyone was curiously staring at me, the new Asian girl, and I was eager for the situation to end. I felt like hiding in a hole, as the cashier rushed me, and the students seemingly mocked me with their white teeth and their white faces. Because it was the beginning of the semester, the only person I knew was my roommate.

In a few minutes, I was saved by a girl who was standing in line behind me, who graciously handed me some cash. She held out her black hand, and smiled at me. I still can't forget her bright, smiling eyes. She and I were a very few minority in the café. She first approached me to help me. Back when I was not familiar with American society, I simply thought that she was a nice black girl. Afterwards, because I was so tired and busy from studying in very different environment, I didn't have a chance to deepen my understanding of the multicultural, the minority issues.

These last few years, as I re-encountered multicultural, minority issues of embedded deeply in American society, I reflected on the hardships I overcame as a member of a minority, and researched the underlying problem. Just as we could never understand the sufferings of a cancer patient unless we experienced the illness ourselves, and as we could never understand the pains of heartbreak if we never experienced it, we could never understand how a minority person feels, living in a white-dominant society.

I had recently reflected on the pains of living as a member of a minority. I surprised even myself, as I felt extremely sorry towards the minority people at a golf club frequented by whites. It felt like the times when I used the tuition money, which my mother had worked so hard for, on mere entertainment, without even studying hard. Especially on my weekly visits to the homeless shelter, I saw the polar opposites of wealth distribution in America, but it pained me further to think that there were also polar opposites of the multicultural, minority problem.

One Thanksgiving, I volunteered at the homeless shelter as I did many other Thursdays. I went to downtown Atlanta while my family was celebrating, to feed the children who were waiting for me at the shelter, so they wouldn't be disappointed. There were a few children at the shelter, and I spent about an hour eating snacks with them and reading to them. The children had eyes brighter than anyone else and were also very smart. I was thankful for the couple hours that I was able to spend with them, as much as I enjoyed spending time with my family. I remembered one line from the Bible that says that as you give more love, you yourself create more love.

I first learned about the multicultural, minority issues in America as I wrote my thesis for my PhD. I learned that education issues in America come from outside of schools and I dug deeper into students' issues at home and the multicultural, minority problems they faced in society. I realized that attempting to simply solve issues of education in school was a futile effort that could never reach the bottom of the problem. The data from a few decades ago showed that the overall US high school graduation rate was only about 60 to 70%. In some large cities, urban high school dropout rates reached 50%. This was like the collapse of the American public school system, and the fact that it could become a societal problem that couldn't even be solved with money piqued my interest.

The majority of inner-city students were black, who often lived with single mothers or guardians. Dropping out of high school leads to the proliferation of already-common youth crimes and continues the cycle of evil in society. The only way to end the cycle is for families and society to take ownership of the problem and look out for the children together.

There were many people who lent their help towards the troubled youths mainly only during the holidays, but the much-needed sustained help still lacked tremendously. The Obama Administration, backed by the firm federal support, established pre-school and kindergarten programs for the minority groups. Thanks to this, single mothers could drop their children off and work federal jobs or continue their education to strive for other jobs, enabling their children to pursue their education more successfully. Also, after-school programs enabled single mothers to be more flexible at work. The lives of many members of minorities were finally stabilized, thanks to these groundbreaking policies, backed by the federal government. That was the climate change of the American environment, and a cultural revolution. It was an excellent example of enlarging a problem in the public schools into the educational and societal spheres in efforts to solve it.

—Jul. 30, 2015

5.2 A Beautiful Quilt Art

At the quilting club I attend sometimes, we make beautiful quilt items and donate them to the people in need, hoping that the pretty blankets will also keep them warm. Quilting is a hard job that requires many small tasks, but when many people work together in a team, all the small pieces come together to complete one amazing piece of art. The finished product is like a representation of all the various races and religions that make up a strong huge American society.

In news and media these days, it seems like the beautiful quilt pattern of American society is being destroyed. With sayings like "Black Lives Matter" and with all the violence and murder, my mind aches as the quilted pattern is distorted. Truthfully, the mosaics may just have been pretty from the outside; maybe the insides were already rotting, ready to spill out. America, based on Puritan beliefs and proponents of capitalism, emphasizes reaching goals and profits, which may have caused the country to overlook the procedures and the causes of the problems.

A few years ago, while working with a volunteer organization, I saw the volunteers sacrificing their valued weekends, cooking warm meals, providing a place to sleep, and even cleaning and kissing the tired feet of the homeless. They truly tried to spread the love of Jesus, as followers. That was a fresh shock to me. It was the true Christian message, to empty one's mind of worldly things.

Maybe what the homeless really needed were loving neighbors who treated them like brothers and sisters, who cooked for them, and cleaned their hurting feet. Instead of mindlessly donating during the holidays, shouldn't we heal the pain of our less fortunate neighbors and share the love of Jesus? Shouldn't American society shift from individualism to a true collectivism with care and consideration for others?

Each of us is different, but if we continue to respect each other and care for our neighbors with the love of Jesus, the slogans of hatred and political extreme division will disappear. Helen Keller once said, "The most beautiful and precious thing in the world is not seen or touched, but can only be felt by the heart." Don't we need true service, love, and caring?

Sometimes I take my dog to the dog park, to let her interact with other dogs without a leash. All the different breeds of dogs play together so well on their first time meeting each other. The German Shepherds, Labs, Chihuahuas, Bulldogs, Beagles, Dachshunds, Poodles, and Yorkies run around, chase each other, and sometimes kiss, playing freely. It is like watching a quilted piece of art in the dog park. The park becomes a calming and enjoyable place and time for me, even if for a brief moment.

— Nov. 10, 2015

5.3 Gun Culture

On a very cold Friday draped with fog and clouds, a dog in a quiet and calm house started barking. An odd odor filled the air. Looking outside, I saw two or three people moving within the fog at the edge of the spacious backyard. They were dressed in gray sweats and because they were wearing hoods over their heads, I could not tell their genders or ethnicities. At first, it seemed as if they were spraying something on the ground; however, after about five minutes, I heard a gunshot. The gunshot rang around the quiet and peaceful backyard, and shook my house and my neighbors'.

Recently in a small town, one of safest place, in the Southern Georgia, an older person sitting on his doorstep in a nearby neighborhood in the town, was shot dead by a young person. Described as murder without reason, this criminal act by criminals has caused some people in their sixties or even older, who have lived their whole lives without guns, to purchase them.

Given this societal environment, the hooded gunmen in my backyard were not an unusual sight. I took a photo of them through my window. No matter how hard I tried, with all the fog, it was difficult to see their identities. It seemed dangerous to check outside, so I called my husband before calling the police. His phone just kept ringing with no response. I also sent a text message. After locking the door shut, I glanced around outside to check their positions before calling 911. After twenty minutes, they were gone from my view. I was scared for my life. I don't like guns. Even if a dangerous situation were to occur, I would never buy a gun.

At dinner in the evening, my husband told me. "Those people who were shooting guns in the backyard – they're my cousins." Infuriated, I angrily asked if they had basic manners. My husband said that they were people with manners, and that it was his mistake. He had told them they could come to our backyard to practice shooting at any time. In the state of Georgia, it is legal to practice shooting within one's own property. Still, it would've been nice if my husband had given me a call or even left a text message giving me a heads up that people will be in the backyard. Carrying and using guns in Americans' daily lives is so different from ones in Korea and is very different culture.

In South Korea, it is assumed that all English teachers know American culture as well as the English language. In reality, I, as an English teacher, gained the different cultural knowledge indirectly through magazines, news, books and movies, and just try to understand American culture through these media. Additionally, this knowledge is not objective many times.

I also only started realizing how much I didn't know about American society while living here. Last year, after police officers were arrested and imprisoned following the Baltimore protests and issues around the Black Lives Matter, movement, I remembered what President Obama said: "Minority rights are yet to be solved and there is still a lot to be done. When I was walking on the streets before I became President, people saw me and started locking their cars in caution." This made me think about the BLM movement on another level and reminded me once again how difficult it is to realize "the multicultural, minority issues." It might be best to follow Carl

Gustav Jung's theories about Collective Unconscious and treat our neighbors with humility and love, without prejudice.

5.4 Remembering the 20th Century's Boxer

When I was a kid, all the boys wanted to be a boxer like Muhammad Ali when they grew up. Muhammad Ali was a world-famous boxer and every Korean boy's role model in 1970s. Because it was a time when various hobbies weren't accessible to young Korean men, they would hang punching bags from ceilings or walls to practice boxing, imitating Ali.

In 1960s, he became a world champion at 18 years old, racking up gold medals and proving he had the hardest punch in the game. Shortly after, he converted to Islam and changed his name to Muhammad Ali from Cassius Marcellus Clay, Jr., criticizing it for being a slave's name. He then participated in the 1960s civil rights movement, raising minority pride and rising against white American dominated society. He followed his religious beliefs in 1966 by actively protesting the Vietnam War.

In 1984, Ali was diagnosed with Parkinson's at 42 and fought the disease for a long time. In the 1996 Atlanta Olympics, he even ran with the torch. When he passed away on June 3rd, 2016 at the age of

74, his funeral was held in his hometown of Louisville, Kentucky.

To my young self, he was just the hero of Korean boys. That he had changed his name, along with his other actions in protest against social injustice, I did not know. Only after living in the United States for a while and further learning about American society did I find out about his background and understand his actions.

In the 1960s, a young man with the hardest punch in the world and a promising future had to face inequality in and alienation from white society, all because of the color of his less-than-1- millemeter-thick skin. He expressed the contradiction with Christianity by protesting the Vietnam War and converting to Islam, and hit America's problematic society with a minority perspective. Muhammad Ali preserved minority pride and threw a hard punch towards the troubled society, showing minority power and pride.

Recently, Michelle Obama said of the White House, "For the past 7 years, it hurt me to open my eyes everyday and think that I lived in a building that slaves once had built." I know very well how lasting the pain, unfelt by perpetrators, is for the victims of minority oppression.

However, I am reminded of the saying that "virtue is paid for by virtue, and resentment is paid for by resilience." Koreans experienced the excruciating pain of colonial rule under Japan for thirty-six years. However, we came to understand Japan's strengths and our weaknesses, and worked hard for a better Korea the past half-century.

There are those who lament over the fact that they were born into white America, much as Michelle Obama was born into a minority group. Regardless, the important thing is to stay resilient and for every American to take after what the Obamas have done in the past 7 years, working hard to fight inequality and discrimination. That beautiful vision is what those from the past and those in the future want.

5.5 Racism

I've previously written about racism, the darkest side of the mosaic that is America, but injustice and inequality towards minorities occurs all over the world. The first generation of many Korean-American immigrants adopt Judeo-Christian, displaying a mixture of Confucian culture and minority characteristics in a white dominated society. For the sake of the next generation, we Koreans must not forsake our own culture in order to pass on a strong cultural climate.

African-Americans seem to maintain their rights in today's American society. Several years ago, a Korean restaurant was sued for including tip on an African-American customer's bill. The restaurant charged a $1.50 tip on a $10.00 bill. There was press release saying it lost millions trying to earn a few dollars. This showcases the customer's tenacity of not letting even the smallest evidence of racism go by, and the united action in African-American community.

The customer felt treated unequally and that it was a question of inequality. I'm sure that the Korean restaurant was upset. It felt that its African-American customers were notorious for not leaving tips, so the owner had charged it without his consent. Americans, unlike Koreans who care a lot about what others think, openly express their opinions. If the food or service is bad, they don't feel the need to tip and no one can say anything. Racial complaints like these incidents have always been prevalent and African-Americans have fought them over the years. They don't look past even small instances like the tip incident. What about us Koreans?

Koreans consider suppressing dissatisfaction as a virtue and see complaints as a negative, even weird. They have unknowingly become used to suppressing emotions in American culture. Many Koreans who settle in America open small businesses. However, it is inevitable that Koreans are Koreans. The next generation will graduate from schools alongside Americans and work alongside them. In order to live and thrive in an American society, Koreans must show the same strength as the African-American community. We must lay a strong foundation so that the next generation can have its own space and equal rights.

There are many organizations that are Korean-focused, and which serve the Korean-American community, often through raising money for scholarships. Scholarships may be important, but it is more critical to recognize and listen to the racial hardships that first- and second-generation Koreans go through on a daily basis.

I'm reminded of a few lines from the poem "Rice" by Seokju Jang. He writes, "Why do people eat? If we live to eat, why do we live?" and I reminisce in embarrassment at the lines

"Promises I should have kept / Things I should have said broken in integrity / Or buried in my throat / A few meals as a reward for those moments".

This fall, I pray that the light shines upon those Korean immigrants who are in the dark.

5.6 Prejudice of The Prejudice

"Preconception" refers to an idea of a person, object, or opinion, that does not come from personal experience, and which we believe without proof. "Prejudice," which is often used as a synonym to preconception, has a more negative connotation; it is a biased, often unfair, thought or idea. It is used often in sociology, where the majority believes a negative, stereotypical assertion of the minority to be true.

William Hazlitt, a famous British author, said that "prejudice is the product of ignorance." Korea is attempting to be a developed country by minimizing societal prejudices. Korean public schools in the past few years, following this trend, have established educational programs that encourage and emphasize diversity and the respect for diversity. By emphasizing the difference, these programs attempt to increase the empathy and favorability towards minority groups of people.

I thought that since America was a country made up of people from different religions, cultures, and values living in harmony like a piece of quilt art, it would not have much prejudice. After living in America for a long time, however, I learned that the country ironically suffered more from the societal issue of prejudice than did other countries. Much of the prejudice existing in society has been there for a long time, trickling down through generations. I thought that many immigrants, including myself, had more exposure to people of different religions, cultures, and values than Americans did, and were thus more likely to view things more rationally, specifically, and objectively.

One day, my husband was saying the pledge of allegiance at school for a ceremony. Everyone was standing except for one person, so the school's leaders were a bit concerned. The singled-out teacher said that he believed his religion came before the school's rules. One day, that teacher had problems with his car, so asked my husband for a ride. My husband who has not had any prejudice against any minority group woke up much earlier than usual, picked his colleague up, and drove to school together. He even postponed his dinner plans to drop his coworker off at his home. I was so curious about the happening and asked my husband what the other teacher was like. He simply said that the teacher "seemed like a good person." It was as if my husband was telling me to not ask any more questions, as the teacher was not much different from anyone else.

My husband doesn't have much prejudice against other people. When he meets disabled people in public, he greets them and shares a few words with them. One young, disabled worker at a restaurant even became friends with my husband and gives us a special family discount every time we eat there. My husband approaches people first with a genuine smile and gentle greetings, extended towards everyone equally. I want to be able to do that as well, but it's not easy.

Recently, very progressive internet media outlets that support Democrats often discuss and criticize people who are prejudiced against homosexuals as homophobes, and people with a prejudice against Islam as Islamophobes. Prejudice should be avoided, but sometimes it can be important to analyze the cause of the prejudice and to attempt to address the solution of the problem related to the prejudice. As Scottish judge and literature critic Francis Jeffrey once said, "Opinions founded on prejudice are always sustained with the greatest of violence."

Americans and people around the world are concerned about, or even afraid of, heightened confrontations and conflicts that are increasingly polarizing. How can we minimize prejudice so we can create a society in which we coexist peacefully? How can we minimize and eradicate the negative cycle of prejudice breeding more prejudice?

The British philosopher John Locke said, "All people complain of societal prejudice as if they are not related to the prejudice. If this is so, what is the solution to these complaints? The only solution to prejudice against others is that all people should reflect themselves first, leaving others behind."

Today, I stand in front of the mirror and think about the philosophies of my husband.

—Jun. 24, 2016

5.7 Repaying Resentment with Righteousness

When I was very little, my father sold his farmland and our house to move to a different region. Because it wasn't a good time to immediately purchase new farmland and a house, we settled in temporary housing and my father held on to some of his cash. However, when an elder at the church was struggling with his business and asked my father for help, my father lent him all of the cash he had, and I had to see my parents go through a tough time when the elder did not repay what he owed.

My father pressed the elder to get his money back for several years. When that didn't work, he tried to just give up and forget it. To this day, my sisters, who were students at the time and whom my father sometimes sent had to ask for the owed money, never borrow anyone's money even if it meant they would starve. My father, who was a minister, never fought legally or physically and seemed to forget about it after waiting patiently. Rather than showing his emotions first, he always judged situations in a composed mindset and went on in a consistent way.

There are many people who are facing hardships in their lives. Violence, murder, war, racial and religious issues caused by selfishness and jealousy; all affect personal lives, seemingly without end. To those who seek religious peace during these times, Christianity and Catholicism point to the love of Jesus and tell us to "love our neighbor as ourselves." Buddhism teaches Buddha's mercy and to be merciful towards the poor and needy. We strive to carry these religious teachings into action, but unless one is a mature adult, it is difficult to do so.

In our traditional religion, Confucius said we should repay resentment with righteousness and goodness. Despite the Nanking Massacre and other atrocities committed by the Japanese during the Sino-Japanese War, it is recorded that the Chinese people looked after thousands of Japanese war orphans and helped the Japanese return home following the war. Simply hating and resenting is unproductive and only breeds more hatred. Therefore, it is important to not lose calmness and handle situations with a righteous view and righteous thinking.

I think the Korean people also repaid the Japanese people's inhumanity and viciousness with righteousness. It is hard to follow the words of Jesus or Buddha to forgive and love all, but I believe we dealt with Japan in a fair way without getting personal. Through trade with Japan, we came to understand their strengths and weaknesses, built up our own weaknesses into new strengths, and became a better Korea.

Currently, the US is headed towards a peak of unforeseen societal confusion due to the US presidential election, racial issues, and religious conflicts. Here, I want to mention Confucius' view and mind. I try to remain calm and handle situations with a righteous eye no matter how much injustice I have faced as a member of a minority group. If I understand others' strengths and improve on my weaknesses, I will become better than them and repay resentment with righteousness.

Confucius' words could heal religious wars in the Middle East and prevent terrorist activities around the world, if only people would listen to them. There is no one perfect in this world. It is important to acknowledge strengths and weaknesses so that the next generation can be courageous and live resiliently. Goodness is controlling one's emotions and carrying into actions with a righteous mindset. This is the driving force behind moving other people, in my vision.

5.8 Garage Sales Stereotypes

A garage sale is an event that takes place when selling their unwanted belongings out of their garage. It usually happens on weekends and is pretty common in America. Advertising for these sales can be found on a local newspaper or on a signs along roads. The price range varies widely but items are usually sold at a huge discount and it's a trustworthy way of purchasing items because you know where the items are from.

Over the past few years, my husband and I have enjoyed stopping by garage sales. Some friends we visited recently also mentioned they frequently visit garage sales too. They then went on to share their experiences with us. They said, "Strangely enough, 99% of antique or garage sale visitors are white. White people seem to be more relaxed and have time for collecting antiques like this." This couple isn't fluent in English and doesn't have time to familiarize themselves with American society and culture. Therefore, they form stereotypes based on external surroundings around them. I felt inclined to do my part and explain further to them about American history, societal norms and culture.

Looking back at African-American history, it is inevitable they lived a desolate life from lack of education and unjust treatment. These factors led to the destruction of families and the straying of children, causing Black society to lag behind for a long period of time. Garage sales mean less to those who have suffered through harmful conditions. I explained to the couple that the reason behind the lack of Black people at garage sales was due to the history of their treatment by US society and government.

It is a pity how long the history of discrimination by skin color has persisted. How distraught must Black scholars have felt after realizing the twistedness of American society? How cynical must they have felt witnessing the contradiction of white supremacy and Christian beliefs? In some ways, black people have carried out God's love more than white people have. They were true Christians who forgave the discriminating white people in the love of God. I wonder if that is why southern Black people are more devout in Christianity. They still live in the south where there has been a history of injustice.

5.9 Black History Month

In the US, February is celebrated as Black History Month. At school, historical videos or movies were shown. I happened to see how White people have historically treated Black people in the US. In restaurants, schools, and residences they were all segregated. All of this took place just because of the color of people's skin. Every time I try to understand Black people's perspective, the inherent contradictions of White racism would not leave my mind.

People say America was a Christian nation established nation under Puritanism, but thinking about the atrocities long time ago, White people committed against Black people makes me think America was full of contradictions in the past. The Bible spreads God's love by telling us to love our neighbors as ourselves. Those Black people who were educated and were aware understood how contradictory White Christian American society was. One example is Muhammad Ali. When the legendary boxer passed away, my husband told me that he was a great boxer but had been labeled a dissident and received public criticism. Once he was awakened after becoming famous, he rebelled against racism by converting to Islam and changing his name to Muhammad Ali.

When I was young in South Korea, I only knew him as an athletic idol and never knew about the back-story of everything. I only found out after living in the US for a while what his actions changing his name meant. I came to understand better the pain black people must have gone through facing racism.

A book that many have read, Gone with the Wind, was famous and loved by readers across the world. I now see that many activists understand it differently since racism issues have been in the center of political, social fields. I also understand better and changed perspective by personally living in the Southern US.

I hope that in Korea, too, people could realize how painful this beautiful work really was. I want to raise the reputation of Black people with Koreans and do something about it the negative stereotypes many Koreans hold. This should be done in a nonviolent way. I do not support destruction, murder and violence. That is because nonviolence is the strongest, most effective, and everlasting method.

When I was young, I put my parents in a difficult position by questioning why I wasn't born prettier or why I didn't have better skin color. When I think about it now, everyone lives with their own types of dissatisfaction. Some things can be resolved but in most instances, one accepts and moves on from the dissatisfaction.

Federal welfare policies, however, can help protect those who are in the dark and left neglected. For example, there are governmental policies in place to accommodate women who are discriminated against in a male-dominated society; or disabled people who need help to adapt themselves to society.

In America, efforts by activists got rid of many bad and racist policies and uplifted the reputation, pride and societal status of Black people. The general public's perspective of Black people have been changed more and better, and those who are aware must work to educate and improve societal stereotypes.

A lesson I have learned through my long years in the US is to acknowledge better Black history, and to change my stereotyped views of how they have been treated. I am so glad I was able to have that opportunity. I am grateful for this change and want to use my talents to get rid of stereotypes in not only American society, but also Korean society.

Chapter VI

Ka-mak-noon, A Modern-Day Illiterate

6.1 The Power of the Press

As society becomes more complex and its problems increase, the importance of the press also increases. Because the living press can also easily rot, its value as society's guide and leader shines through. Sohn Suk-hee is synonymous with the Korean press. When the authorities were rotting, Sohn courageously reported for the citizens and displayed the prosperity of our press.

In 2009, American broadcaster Glenn Beck exposed hidden truths through Fox News to US homes every night. He glued many Americans to their televisions, with "raw news straight from the source before it got taken down on the Internet by the authorities." One incident was the mass shooting of November 2009, in Fort Hood military base. 13 people, including Army medical personnel, were killed. The White House and the CIA first reported this incident as "violence in the workplace." Many Americans and politicians believed it, too. However, Glen Beck and Fox News, after continued research, reported that the incident at Fort Hood was not a simple case of violence in the workplace. Beck pressured Congress and the administration in D.C. to form an official team to conduct strict investigations in the matter. Finally, weeks after the shooting, the group reinvestigated and concluded that it was not, in fact, a simple act of violence; the incident was a pre-planned murder and an act of terrorism by shooter Nidal Hasan, a US Army major. This uncovering was thanks to the press reporting against the power of authorities.

In 2012, US ambassador Christopher Stevens and 8 employees were killed at the US embassy in Benghazi, Libya. At first, right after the event, the White House, CIA, UN Leaders, and the Democratic Party all agreed that a Muslim soldier set a fire at the embassy, after being enraged by an anti-Islam film. News press around the world agreed with the story. Again, Fox News diligently researched and reported, convincing the Republican Party to organize another government-sponsored investigative team. Two weeks of careful investigations later, the group found out that the Department of Foreign Affairs and the White House refused to send additional security personnel, despite the embassy having said countless times that it felt imminent danger. Stevens and his 8 employees were gruesomely murdered by organized terrorists.

One journalist exposed the truth to 300 million Americans. Thanks to Beck, Fox News peaked in its popularity, leading NBC and CNN to advertise on Fox for viewership just like the Korean most popular newscaster, Mr Sohn and his broadcasting team did. British magazine *The Guardian* says that its reporters work hard to always search for new stories, using small coffee shops in each local area and the company is able to deliver the fastest truth to the British as well as to everyone else in the world.

Recently, attention has been focused on Brussels, where the EU Headquarters is located, because of a terrorist attack. However, *The Guardian* says that, "someone uploaded an older violent video, not filmed directly in Brussels, on YouTube, and a renowned news agency reported that it was live footage." Another news agency copied the renowned news agency's report and broadcast it again. Through these incidents, we realize how important it is for the press to deliver the truth to the people.

6.2 Hackers' Hidden War

I first used a computer in 1986 when I started teaching. It was much more expensive than computers are now, and I remember using it to do schoolwork and writing thesis. Since then I have had an inseparable relationship with computers, and they have become an important part of my life. Events in the past few years, though, have completely turned my love for computers into hate.

For example, my computer was hacked into and I lost my dissertation draft that I had been working on for a year. A professional who had worked in the IT team of the United States Military, arguably a top talent in his field, told me that, because highly skilled hacker touched it, I wouldn't be able to use the computer again nor recover my dissertation draft.

Recently, hackers' crimes have evolved. Often times, money from banks disappears and leaving no trace. The medical field is affected too, since most of our personal medical information is saved online, and we are prone to identity theft. In 2009, the Korean government was taken down by a DDoS attack and was affected badly. American

IRS and Social Security are vulnerable from hackers, either. Sometimes we are the victims of identity theft from the backdoor transactions of IT companies.

Security issues are around us all the time. I search for items to buy on Google a couple times, they keep popping up on their recommended ads as my favorites in Google as well as on other search engines. At first I was amazed and excited. But the more I think about it, the more horrible it seems that someone is organizing my likes and dislikes online. These days, bank burglars don't attack with guns. The hackers quietly break through the bank's security system and with their fingers alone steal millions. People with large bank accounts don't even realize that thousands have been taken from their accounts.

The word "hacker" used to carry a negative connotation, but now, governments and businesses publicly employ "white hackers"; hackers employed by those with money and power to look for weakness in networks. Even important government facilities aren't free from the corruption and dangers within networks. A few years ago, there was a report that said supercomputers used in governments and international corporations were sold with spyware chips used in information wars. That meant that a powerful nation could easily access and affect another weaker country's atomic facilities, military facilities, and various intelligence databases.

Thus, national security depends on hackers or the nations' abilities to hire these top hackers. The problem is the question of conscience and morality. In modern society, large accidents happen when the people controlling the networks don't act morally. However, the power to run networks is usually hidden away from the public eye. Most of us wouldn't know if an innocent person could be blamed for a hacking crime by manipulating.

The network users who have become addicted to convenience are unknowingly moving towards a new global order. The world can move at the fingertips of evildoers if the evils have a network's power. Currently, American companies holds the network's key technology as well as Microsoft's Windows system. After realizing America's dominance, according to a newspaper reporter, Putin of Russia seven years ago ordered his aides to use 19th century typewriters. This level of security might help Russia helped how he recently won the war in Syria against the so-called terrorist rebels.

Sometimes, I go for walks in a forest, near a pond. The pretty green leaves twinkling in the sunlight are like a springtime symphony. The pond is so placid that it softly ripples from the movement of little insects. I stop for a bit and peer into the pond. Unlike on the calm surface, there is a quiet raging war underwater: minnows looking for food and other fish hunting the minnows; just like the hackers who fight wars secretly and quietly in hidden places for astronomical amounts of money and power.

6.3 What is True

After the terrorist attack of 9/11 in which 5000 lives were lost, President Bush, with Congress's and the nation's full support, invaded Iraq to catch the terrorists and created a detention camp in Guantanamo Bay.

However at the end of his second term, Bush was hit with a shoe of an audience at one of his speeches. A group of Anonymous hackers reported that there were civilian casualties during the invasion in Iraq, making the world question the Bush Administration's legitimacy and celebrate the heroism of the Anonymous group. Even students in Korea discussed about Bush's faults.

Courageously, when Bush's presidency ended, The Anonymous group accused the new Obama's government of another corruption: that the government was spying on its good citizens using Big Data. Anonymous members, Assange and Snowden, were no longer considered heroes, but the most dangerous people in the world.

Same actions can have vastly different consequences under the direction of governmental powers. Yesterday's hero can be today's traitor. The written record of history depends on who is writing it. The fragments of real news often disintegrate and prominent members of the compilation committees who are supportive to the political power, have "created" the history of the world. Why don't the truths of events become known and get recorded as they happen?

Thus, History was always my least favorite subject in my school years. I couldn't understand why we had to memorize the events of the past and get tested on them. On the other hand, I was intrigued by subjects like sports, math, and science, in which one had to rely on truth and rules to arrive at a conclusion. Those classes were always refreshing to me. I could simply follow the rules and formulas to get the correct answer, easily getting a good grade, A, without studying too hard. It is very easy to get a right answer as long as one can think reasonably and logically.

As I get older, I realized that our society doesn't move neatly according to rules and formulas like in sports or science. I get into endless debates over the subject of the truth, so I close my mouth and try to keep silent. In a meeting last year, someone said to me as I worried over current societal and political happenings, "if I have food in my mouth, I don't care about whatever happens outside." At the time I lamented his thought, but honestly, most people live that way.

It seems like people talk of conscience and ethics only after they have food in their mouths, whether they are Christian, Buddhist, religious leaders, ordinary people, or not. It does not matter much on what is true over what is happening now in our lives. Perhaps that's why many people own dogs. They care and look out for their owners first directly and faithfully. They never change their faithful to owner.

6.4 Secrets and The Corruption

Secrets often have a negative connotation. Especially when it's a top secret, even darker and more serious evils may underlie it. I was in sixth grade when I first discovered the world of secrets.

I had graduated from elementary school, and it was the first day of middle school. I left my house excitedly, wearing the new clothes and shoes that I had picked out the night before. It was a co-ed school, and we girls said to each other that the 6th grade boys had weirdly changed. The boys had indeed changed from the ones we had known in elementary school, appearing with hormonal acne, sparse mustache, and the strange looks in their eyes when they looked at girls.

When I walked in, the student council was inspecting everyone's attire to check that hair, uniforms, name-tags, and shoes were all fit to school regulations. Past the main gate in the south wing, there was a small restroom building. I was walking by it to go to my classroom when I saw seven male students standing by a corner, frozen with fear. Three bigger boys were threatening the smaller boys, punching and kicking them relentlessly.

For the first time in my life, I was glad that I was born a girl because, at the time, there were no violent female gangs. In the 1970s, people carefully watched their words, since there was no saving them from gangsters. The gang members had blood alliances, so not even families and friends knew about the groups. Parents just hoped that their sons kept their distance from these dangerous gang members.

I noticed that another example of secret group activities when I first started teaching in the late 80s. One wise and brave PE teacher in my school was lecturing a male student for a long time in the teachers' office. That student was a gang member, and the teacher, bearing a huge risk, advised the student to leave the gang group. The boy, though he did suffer physical trauma, was able to leave the gang organization and eventually graduate from middle school. The first code of these gangs is, "Don't Ask, Don't Tell." That's why these cancerous organizations don't disappear easily and continued to spread to other cities.

In recent, the American CIA's code, "Don't Ask, Don't Tell." has reminded me of the bad experiences.

We have seen and learned many times in the history that when agencies holding top secrets become corrupt, they can lead to terrible, unimaginable conditions to our local community, government, and world.

—Jan. 26, 2017

6.5 Wells Fargo's Ghost Accounts

Wells Fargo is one of the largest American financial institutions, specializing in home and personal loans, and has a long history. My husband's salary is automatically deposited to this bank, and it is also the bank widely used by federal and state government workers.

Recently, by Foxnews report, a massive fraud by the bank was uncovered, of an unprecedented scale. Wells Fargo made 2 million "ghost" accounts, using its customers' personal information without permission. This was a huge fraud crime. It should have resulted in a criminal case in court, not a civil case. Because of these ghost accounts, customers' credit scores could be adversely affected. Because of this case, 5,300 Wells Fargo employees were fired too. I don't believe that the employees voluntarily created those ghost accounts. Some of them were probably heads of families, but had their jobs snatched away because of this storm of a large wrong doing work.

It seemed like too coincidental. Female reporter and lawyer, Greta Van Sustain, at Foxnews was covering aggressively the story but suddenly she said she was stepping down from her job. For these large fraud case, the heads of organizations probably ordered or initiated the crimes, and those on the lower end just had to follow the orders, but they were the ones whose jobs were on the line. The authorities at the top of the chain have so much power but once the crime was exposed, they were busy blaming the weaker ones in the chain. Greta at Foxnews passionately reported that this was why the American politics downplayed the crime to be a civil case and resorted to charging Wells Fargo a small fine.

The U. S. Consumer Financial Protection Bureau, CFPB, charged a fine. US Senate Banking & Financing Committee also released to the press that this case had been disclosed to the public because Wells Fargo's employees demanded that there should have been a fair treatment to them. Before the consequences got more serious and the case came before the House Financial Services Committee meeting on September 29, 2015, the board of directors at Wells Fargo decided to force the remuneration amount, apart from stocks, from two CEOs. As long as the corrupt powers continue to exist, it seemed like the blame did only reach the weaker of the strong power.

To be honest, as I saw this crime case unfold at Wells Fargo, I thought that it was bound to happen. After the election in 2009, many banks reformed, including Wells Fargo's revolutionary internal reform. As a long-time customer, I immediately sensed the change in bad ways. The friendly bank tellers who worked at the window or the drive-through suddenly disappeared because of the bank reforms. This was also the time when many Americans lost ownership of their homes in that period because they couldn't repay the banks' interests, called house crises.

Ordinary American citizens lost their homes. The middle class started to collapse. When it saw that large financial institutions were troubled by their foreclosed homes, the federal government released a large homeowners' loan. With the home loan, the new bank systems prioritized lower-income people, in moving into these newly foreclosed homes. As a result, the traditional American middle class was unable to repay its loans and lost their homes.

Well Fargo bank's case was not surprising to me in that the people at the top of the organization dodged the net of the law and merely had to pay only small fines.

— Sep. 28, 2016

6.6 The Convenience Trap

In modern society, we rely on the convenience of internet and network. But the convenience can blind us to the problems that computer and internet can cause.

For the first time in about a year, I went to a golf club in my city to practice for a game I have in a couple of days. I had reserved a spot online and paid for the golf cart and the greens fees with my credit card. A young male worker there said that since the course was quiet after 11:30, I could come in any time after that to practice. So, I met a friend at 10:00, got some work done, and then went to the golf club after 11:30.

When I went to the golf club to check in, a female worker there said that I was checked in already. Baffled, I said to her that a male employee in the club told me that I could come practice any time after 11:30, so I came in late after finishing up some personal work. The worker said that she could not help me since I was checked in already. I retorted by saying that since there were surveillance cameras around, we could check who had checked in earlier under my name. After chatting with her manager, the employee checked me in. Wanting to find out what had happened, I called the manager the next day. Apparently, it was a small glitch in the system. The small mistake in networking system made many people confused.

Also, there is other example of bad side of technology. Fox News reporters Bill Hemmer and Martha MacCallum stated in a report that "using algorithms, Facebook blocks positive news about the conservative Republican Party, but spreads positive news about the Democratic Party." I have noticed this about Facebook for the past few years, so this report seems a bit behind the times to me. The internet tremendously influences our daily lives, and the sphere of influence of a forum like Facebook is almost unfathomable. But perhaps even Facebook can't escape from the power game.

In addition, regarding the posting of my weekly column, an acquaintance recently called me, and asked,

"Why don't you write columns anymore?"

"I'm not sure what you mean." I answered.

"I write columns every week and check every Friday on the email newsletter."

To this, he replied in disbelief,

"I used to read the newsletter everyday",

"but I haven't seen the *Dr. Kwon's Column* for the past four weeks, since your *Area 51* column."

I told him about something I experienced last April:

"I also used to read my column every Friday on the online newsletter, but one week I didn't see my work. Thinking that this was strange, I double-checked the date and the region. Turns out, sometimes the Atlanta issue is delivered as the LA issue or the NewYork issue, and that's why you might not see my column."

"This may happen due to someone's mistake or oversight, so you always have to check that it's the Atlanta issue first!"

After that, I sent him 4 weeks' newsletters containing my columns. My columns mostly cover political, social issues. Thankful for my readers' engagement, I try ever-harder to write better and more thoughtful stories.

All three things above are related to our uses of computer and internet. I hope that in the shadow of the convenience, there are no network errors, or worse, intentional manipulations.

6.7 Sanctuary City

The term "sanctuary" is familiar to me as a Christian, because places of worship are often referred to as sanctuaries. Recently, a similar term "sanctuary city" has been showing up in the conservative media against left lean politics. The dictionary definition of "sanctuary city" is "a place separate from the ordinary world, in which the sacred spirit is believed to be held."

In the media, however, "sanctuary city" refers to a specially protected area in which the American government protects and supports refugees. According to a news report, the US Immigration Office officially took in 100 Christians and 10,000 Muslims in 2016. In addition, it even took efforts to create sanctuary cities in which war refugees were protected and legally able to reside in the country.

According to one of conservative news outlets, Fox News, refugees residing in these sanctuary cities have committed many crimes of rape, kidnapping, and murder, in public places. The police have contacted the sanctuary cities to help the victims and to investigate the facts, but the government has limited police intervention in the area. American citizens have suffered in extreme anxiety and fear.

The fact that Trump won the presidential elections recently and that the Republican Party filled positions in the general election could be attributed to the decreasing trust and confidence that American citizens have in the government. Did most voters not expect Trump and the Republican Party to make America safer and restore its order? Trump has declared that he strictly opposes the crimes committed by illegal immigrants and any criminal activities residing in sanctuary cities.

We will have to wait and see what actions Trump will take for the criminals from the sanctuary cities, in order for them to follow American laws and standards.

— Nov. 9, 2019

6.8 Brexit 2.0

"Brexit" means that Britain is exiting the European Union (EU). The EU not only burdened the British citizens financially, but it also pressured the country to loosen its refugee situation, to the point that it was jeopardizing the safety of the country. In response, Britain held a nation wide referendum, and decided to exit the EU to autonomously improve the country's safety. Especially when the country was requested to open up its borders for countless more Muslim refugees and to provide further economic safeguards for them, British citizens chose to leave the EU, to protect their families from potential violence, murder, and terror.

In the United States, a similar situation ensued, as Republican Donald Trump was elected president. I like to refer to this as Brexit 2.0. The Obama administration's globalization policy was based on anti-Christianity and anti-capitalism. Because the government took in so many Muslim refugees and illegal immigrants, American citizens felt that their safety and lives were threatened. Older citizens, who lived their entire lives without the need for guns, started purchasing them in the past few years for survival. It was publicly regarded that

America was not a safe place to live anymore. Furthermore, because of Obamacare, the middle class saw its healthcare costs multiply, and people felt that their lives were threatened. The situation was exacerbated by the decrease in the middle class, as half of Americans were living as part-time workers.

While looking for the next leader to ensure safety and financial stability in America, the middle class noticed Donald Trump in the live TV debates. To them, Trump was a tall, healthy, seemingly honest, and average man. He was not eloquent like professional politicians, but in his authentic manner, he stated his claims. A graduate of the New York Military Academy and the Wharton School of the University of Pennsylvania, Trump thought the same way as the average citizen did. He promised to regain the social order by differentiating between people who immigrated to the nation legally and those who did so illegally; to improve the medical system to help those who were suffering from the high medical costs arising from Obamacare; and to help everyone live affluently, just as he had.

Trump policies were certainly alluring to everyone who heard them. The promise to eradicate the terrorist attacks and to raise America's dignity connected with the American wishes. On the other hand, Hillary Clinton's policy to open the American borders and to continue Obamacare seemed no different from the current administration's policies.

Opinion polls and the voting atmosphere favored Clinton. However, laborers, African Americans, Hispanics, women, and White Americans who disagreed with the current administration voted for Trump and the Republican party. The wish to improve individual safety peaked and the election had the turnout of the century, marking Trump's win. The votes that the American petit bourgeoisie casted on Trump was perhaps a second Brexit, one that related to a person's most basic needs of safety and survival.

6.9 The Silent Majority vs. the Loud Minority

At first, I thought it was odd that Americans naturally smiled and said hi to strangers, because if you do so in South Korea, people think you are unwell. If a man acted that way, most women would be cautious, at least initially. When I came to America to study in 1997, however, I realized that it was Southern American culture to smile and say "hi," everywhere and every time, from walking on the streets, to riding the elevator, to strolling in the park. I thought that Americans were very friendly, and that citizens in an advanced country were something different. It was also very common for drivers to yield to each other. My first impression of America was that its citizens were born to be kind, and that beautiful nature like deer and birds surrounded us.

In the last seven or eight years, however, the American society felt a strong gust of the wind of change. The campaign slogan for Obama was even: "Change, you can do it." The first change I personally noticed was the increase of large trucks speeding in the 1st and 2nd lanes on the highway. Trucks the size of the one used in the Berlin truck attack are speeding past not in the third or fourth lanes, but in the first and second lanes ruthlessly. Several times, I thought that my small car was going to flip over from the wind created by speeding trucks. Also, on the streets, at the bank, or at the shops, people who used to smile and say hi now reluctantly raise their eyes from their computers and cell phones, after I say hi first. I am often surprised at how much American society has changed, compared to a few years ago.

The changes also occurred in places that I never thought would. According to public policy, now the greeting that we have used for a long time, "Merry Christmas," around Decembers is no longer acceptable in public under Obama administration. We are encouraged to use more neutral language, such as "Happy Holidays," in public.

In the last few years, oppression of Christianity has occurred in Middle Eastern countries, as well as in the Philippines, Malaysia, India, and Africa. In the United States and Europe, the power of the anti-Christian Islamic brotherhood expands under the euphemism of "globalization." In this changing America, the majority of the citizens are silent. What are the politicians doing to win their hearts? The most important thing is to be on the people's side.

Republican Donald Trump is famous for using Twitter often. He connected with citizens by proudly saying "Merry Christmas" in front of a Christmas tree. The press and the Obama White House acted as loud spokespeople for the minority and failed to listen to the silent majority. Trump read the majority's minds, and communicated through Twitter. The result was gaining their hearts.

— Dec. 22, 2016

6.10 *Ka-Mak-Noon*, A Modern-Day Illiterate

In the town I lived in when I was little, there was an old lady who did not know how to read. Every once in a while, she would come to our house with letters and documents, and ask us for help. She was illiterate. The woman's children could get by lying to her about their report card grades, even if the grades were bad. According to the dictionary, *ka mak noon* refers to "illiterate, a person who cannot read, as figurative expression," as well as "one who is unaware about anything."

After the 36 year Japanese colony and the Korean War, Koreans suffered economic hardship as well as social unease, and its literacy rates, as a result, were very low. In the 1970s, to increase literacy, the government implemented the New Community Movement, called *Sae Ma Eul*, educating citizens, creating new jobs, and awarding scholarships to top students. At the time, there were a lot of illiterates, but now, only 50 years later, Korea boasts the world's highest college graduation rate. I feel very proud whenever I read articles that tell stories of overcoming the "Illiterate Age," written by people in their 70s and 80s.

However, there are many kinds of illiteracy in the modern age. Because many areas of knowledge are now segmented and very specialized, a lot of new kinds of illiterate persons have surprisingly surfaced. For example, I drive my car every day, but I don't know anything about the mechanisms of my car. If I think about it, there are many things that I use every day, yet have no knowledge of. When an item breaks, I can't do anything without the help of a professional: I am a modern-day "illiterate of motor tech."

When that illiterate runs or manages a company or an organization, a bigger problem than we can imagine occurs. One example is the email hacking of Hillary Clinton, former Secretary of State. More seriously, the hacking of the emails could have potentially jeopardized the personal information of 30 million Americans. In this advanced, information society with high technology, if people are illiterate about issues of technology, they will unknowingly suffer like the old ladies of Korea in the 1960s and 1970s like being *Ka-Mak-Noon*. Thus, especially, more frequent uses of highly advanced technology in politics between parties, organizations, or governments could caused much more seriously bad impacts.

— Apr. 22, 2017

ISBN 979 - 11 - 90121 - 46 - 0

Edited by An hye-sook
Book design by Lim jung-ho

Printed by Jinsol CTP, Inc., in Republic of Korea.
First printing, 2023.

Literature Consciousness
939, Ganghwa-daero,
Hajeom-myeon, Ganghwa-gun,
Incheon, Republic of Korea